"Lindy, I should pr

"Do you want to go?"

That was a loaded question if ever Zeke heard one. "My bottle's empty."

She licked her lips. "So is my glass. Do you want another one?"

"No. I don't."

"Then what *do* you want?"

That was a tricky question, because what he wanted didn't come in a bottle. Or a glass.

He touched a finger to the polish on one of her toes. "I want to be like this nail polish. I want to be wild. Just because I can. Isn't that what you said?"

"Yes," she whispered.

"So what if I did something wild…like kiss you?"

"Then I might have to do something a little wild, too. Like kiss you back."

And with that, he did something he'd been wanting to do ever since that day in his office. He drew her close and planted his mouth on hers.

Dear Reader,

Those of you who have children know how scary life can sometimes be. Each time my kids coughed or sneezed or had an ache or pain, my mind would invariably choose door number three, aka Worst. Case. Scenario. My family laughs over my uncanny ability to make a diagnostic mountain out of a medical molehill.

But those mountains do exist. And pediatric surgeon Zeke Bruen faced that mountain and crashed and burned on the other side of it. After the tragic loss of his daughter, he sank into a pit that cost him his marriage and he can't bear the thought of going through that kind of pain again.

Then along comes Lindy Franklin and her daughter, Daisy, and they turn his world upside down. Not only is Daisy unbearably cute and sweet, but Lindy has endured a completely different kind of tragedy that raises his protective instincts to an all-time high.

Thank you for joining Lindy and Zeke as they traverse those mountains and attempt to make peace with what they can't change.

I hope you enjoy reading this couple's journey as much as I loved writing it!

Love,

Tina Beckett

A FAMILY TO HEAL HIS HEART

TINA BECKETT

HARLEQUIN® MEDICAL ROMANCE™

Recycling programs
for this product may
not exist in your area.

ISBN-13: 978-1-335-64172-4

A Family to Heal His Heart

First North American Publication 2019

Copyright © 2019 by Tina Beckett

Printed in U.S.A.

To my children, who put up with my absurd
schedule, and who love me in spite of it.

CHAPTER ONE

LINDY FRANKLIN'S PULSE HAMMERED, and she swiped at the alarm clock to silence it, just as she had every morning for the last two years, before falling back onto the bed in relief. Six o'clock. Just like always. Only now there was no reason to leap up and try to rush to Daisy before she woke up and started to cry. No reason to make omelets and toast for her husband. But she still needed to get up, or her mom would arrive, and she'd be late for her new job.

An actual paying job this time.

Moving back to Savannah had been the right thing to do. Even if admitting she'd been wrong was one of the hardest things she'd ever done. So had realizing that most of her old friends had moved on with their lives. And who could blame them?

Climbing out of bed and sliding her feet into a pair of fuzzy slippers, she went into the bathroom, where the words taped to her mirror caught her eye.

"New beginnings, Lindy. New beginnings." She recited the phrase just as she had every morning. Ever since the judge had told her she was free to leave Fresno—and her old life—behind.

Today really was a new beginning for her. For the first time since the move to California she'd be able to practice medicine again. Her marriage had closed the door to a lot of things. Her release from it was slowly opening them back up again.

Mouthing her mantra one more time, she hurriedly showered and got dressed and fixed Daisy's breakfast.

The doorbell rang, and she froze for a pained second. Then she laughed. It was just her mom coming to pick up Daisy.

She swung it open and there stood Rachel Anderson, as tall and elegant as ever.

"You're early. I was just about to get her up."

"I know. I wanted to make sure I was here in plenty of time."

"You always are." She grinned and drew her mom into the house. "I don't think you've been late a day in your life."

Unlike Lindy, who tended to run just a few minutes behind no matter how hard she pushed herself. It had been one of those "failings" that had been used as a hammer.

New beginnings.

"I'm not sure that's true, sweetheart."

She was pretty sure it was. But her mom's sweet southern drawl spelled home the way nothing else ever had. She wrapped her in a tight hug.

"What was that for?"

"Just for being you."

Her mother had been a huge help in making sure she got back on her feet, first by watching Daisy while Lindy had volunteered at the women's crisis center. And now by insisting she apply for the nursing position at Mid Savannah Medical Center.

Lindy drew a deep breath. "I'll get Daisy. And I've just put breakfast on the table. Do you want something?"

"No, and I told you I could fix Daisy breakfast at the house."

"I know you did. But I want to try to keep things as normal as possible for her, since I'll be away from home a lot longer than I was before."

Normal. What a beautiful word. She'd only recently realized just how beautiful it was.

"And you will." Rachel peered into her daughter's face. "How are you holding up?"

"Good, Mom. Good. It's just been crazy, trying to get settled in the new house. I didn't expect to get an answer on the job so soon."

Her husband had left her one good thing: a life insurance policy that had helped her coast along. It had made her squirm to take the money, but that money had also paid for therapy and sundry other things.

Mid Savannah Medical Center had asked about the three-year lapse since her last position in Georgia, but she'd covered by saying she'd taken some time off to be home with her daughter. Not exactly a lie. She'd gotten a surprise phone call the next day telling her she had her dream job as a surgical nurse in the pediatric ward. Her parents had cosigned for the loan on her little starter home—since she hadn't had a job at the time. She'd vowed to herself that she'd make them proud.

"I told you it wouldn't take long. Maybe you should have waited a little while longer before getting back out there. I'm sorry if I rushed you into applying."

She gave her mom's hand a squeeze. "You didn't. I needed to do something, and this was the perfect opportunity."

Her mom was a music professor at one of the local colleges. She'd been alarmed when Lindy had told her she wasn't going back to work after getting married. She'd been right to be concerned, because Luke had wanted to pack up and move to Fresno almost immediately, effectively isolating her from everyone and everything she'd known.

But that was all water under the bridge. She was back, and she intended to stay back. Nothing or no one would ever change that again.

"Why don't you let me get Daisy ready? I

promise I'll lock the doors behind me when I leave."

She hesitated. Locking the doors herself had become her own personal ritual. One she wasn't sure she was ready to give up. But she'd have to sometime. And the last thing she wanted was to give her mom more cause to worry. "Are you sure you don't mind?"

"No. It'll give me and my granddaughter some time to bond before heading out."

Lindy's chest ached. Living on the other side of the country meant that her mom hadn't seen Daisy until she'd moved back home. Not for lack of trying. Luke had thought of every reason under the sun why her parents couldn't come to see them, though: the house was too small; the trip would be too hard on them; he couldn't spare the time away from work.

Those days were behind her now. And her parents had already spent the last two years getting to know Daisy. And Daisy— maybe because of how young she was—had adapted to her new life quickly. Her daughter hadn't asked once about her father, for which Lindy was truly grateful.

"I think you bonded the moment she saw you and Daddy. But thank you." She glanced at her phone. She still had twenty-five minutes to get to work, but Savannah traffic could be unpredictable. "Maybe I can be on time for once in my life. Hopefully they'll like me."

"Just be yourself, honey. They're all going to love you. How could they not?"

And with those words ringing in her ears, she scooped up her keys, gave her mom a kiss on the cheek and hurried out the door.

Zeke Bruen was not loving the new surgical nurse. She'd done nothing wrong and was on top of every request almost before he asked, but he'd seen her eyes repeatedly stray toward the big clock on the wall. Counting down the hours until she was with her husband? Boyfriend?

Gritting his teeth, he ignored those thoughts. Some people did have a life outside the hospital. He certainly didn't expect everyone on his team to be like he was. But when they were here, he expected them to be present. Especially when it was a certain person's first day on the job.

Things had been so rushed getting into the surgical suite that he hadn't had a chance to introduce himself, although he'd been told the new nurse's name as he'd scrubbed in: Lindolynn Franklin. So maybe someone had told her his as well. Well, it wouldn't hurt to have a little chat with her after they were done here.

And do what, Zeke? Confront her about looking at the clock?

He looked too, but it was to keep track of whether things were going as expected.

Maybe Nurse Franklin was doing the same thing. Somehow he didn't think so. Those glances had seemed furtive and once, when she'd caught his eye afterward, color had flooded into the portion of her face visible above her surgical mask. The sight had turned his stomach inside out. That certainly hadn't helped.

Returning his attention to his patient with an irritated shrug, he busied himself with reconnecting the pulmonary artery, making sure each tiny stitch he placed was secure. The last thing he needed was to close this little girl's chest and have the repair leak.

A half-hour later he was done, giving a nod to each of his team with murmured thanks. Then he left the room and stripped off his gloves, relief washing through him. He'd done this particular surgery dozens of times, but each time he cracked open a child's chest, a moment of doubt threatened to paralyze him. He'd always gotten over it, his muscle memory taking over until he could get his mind back in the game. Maybe that's what had happened with the new nurse. The only thing to do was feel her out.

He propped a shoulder against the wall outside the double doors as the surgical team slowly filed out, many of them congratulating him. That wasn't what he was waiting for, however. He was searching for an unfamiliar face.

There. Her eyes connected with his for an instant before she attempted to veer off in the other direction. Good try. He fell into step beside her. "Sorry. I didn't get a chance to introduce myself before we got started."

He held out a hand. "Ezekiel Bruen."

"Oh, um, I'm Lindy Franklin. I'm new here."

Lindy. That fit. As did the rest of her face, now that her mask was gone. Delicate bones and the subtle curve of her cheeks gave her a breakable air that made him uneasy, and he had no idea why.

"So I've heard." He thought for a second she was going to ignore his outstretched hand, but then she stopped walking and placed hers in it, the light squeeze reaffirming his musings and making him hesitate. Maybe he shouldn't say anything.

And if it had been another member of his team?

He stiffened his resolve, determined to keep things professional. "I noticed you were in a rush to get out of surgery. Not happy with where the administration placed you?"

"What? Oh…no. I mean yes." That vibrant color he'd seen in the operating room reappeared, only this time he was actually able to watch as it flowed up her cheeks before receding like an ocean wave. "Why would you think I was in a hurry to get out of there?"

He ignored the quick tightening of his gut. "You were watching that clock pretty closely."

The pink returned, darker this time, and white teeth sank into a full lower lip. "I was just…" She paused as if trying to figure out how to explain herself. "I didn't realize I was. And I'm perfectly happy with where I've been placed."

So she wasn't going to let him in on whatever had kept her mind so occupied.

Well, if that's the way she wanted to play it… "As long as you're up to the demands of working with the surgical staff."

Her back stiffened, and her chin angled up. Light brown eyes rimmed with dark lashes met his head on. "I am quite up to the demands. Thank you for your concern, though."

That show of strength made him smile.

It wasn't a true thank you, and they both knew it. But he'd gotten his message across.

Time to revert to his normal, friendly self. If it even existed anymore.

"Have you been in town long?"

"I was born and raised here in Savannah." The slightest flicker of her eyelids said there was something more to that story.

"So was I." He studied her for a second. "Did you transfer here from one of the other hospitals?"

"No."

So much for being friendly. He guessed it was none of his business where she'd come from. She could have just graduated from nursing school for all he knew. But the way she'd handled those instruments said she knew her way around an operating room. That kind of self-assurance only came with experience. But if she hadn't transferred from one of the local hospitals, where had she gained that experience? Unless she actually did have something to hide. Some kind of mistake that hadn't shown up on her résumé? He didn't want to go digging through her past or call her previous place of employment, but maybe he should. Just so he'd be aware of any issues before they cropped up and became a problem here. Or maybe he should just ask her outright.

"Where did you practice before this, then?" He could have asked Human Resources, but he wanted to see if she would balk about answering.

She named a place in the heart of Savannah.

"I thought you said you didn't transfer."

"I didn't." She gave a quick shrug. "I took a few years off and then decided I couldn't live without nursing."

She'd taken a few years off...

It hit him all of a sudden. His glance went to her ring finger. It was empty, but he was pretty sure there was an indentation there where a ring had once been. So she'd been married, but wasn't any longer? She could have taken some time off during that relationship, but he had a feeling he knew what had caused her inordinate interest in that clock. "I take it you have a child."

Her mouth popped open and then closed again, the color that had seeped into her face disappearing completely. "How did you know?"

"Just a hunch. The clock-watching had to be for a reason. And you took 'a few years off.' I wasn't trying to pry."

"It's okay. She's three. It's my first time leaving her with anyone for this length of time."

Including the child's father? Something about that made the hair on the back of his neck stand up, although it was ridiculous. Maybe the man had traveled so much that there'd never been time to leave her with him or with anyone else. Or maybe the mark on her finger was a figment of his imagination.

It was also none of his business.

She gave a quick shake of her head as if reading his thoughts before meeting his gaze again. "Well, it was nice working with you, Dr. Bruen—"

"Call me Zeke. Everyone does."

"Okay…" She drew the word out like it made her uncomfortable. Did she think he was hitting on her? Damn. Nothing could be further from the truth, despite that quick jerk to his senses after seeing her without her surgical mask for the first time. He hadn't felt that since… Well, in quite a while.

Time to put her mind at ease, if that were the case.

"We're pretty informal here at Mid Savannah."

"I guess I'm not used to that. You can call me Lindy, then."

"What's your daughter's name?" He had no idea why he asked that, and the last thing he should be doing was talking about baby girls with anyone. He never encouraged his colleagues to talk about their children, and most of the old-timers knew why. Maybe it was because of how reticent she'd been to talk to him. About anything.

"Her name is Daisy."

Daisy. He liked that. His own daughter's name had been Marina.

A shaft of pain arced through him and then was gone.

"Nice name."

"Thank you."

His glance went past her to see Nancy, one of the OR nurses, coming up the corridor, heading for them. She touched Lindy on the shoulder, only to have her give a squeak and nearly jump out of her skin. She whirled to the side, face white, eyes wide. She seemed to go slack when she saw who it was.

Her fellow nurse frowned. "Sorry. I didn't mean to scare you." She held up a phone. "Is this yours? It was left on the desk."

"Oh! Yes, it is. Thank you." She suddenly grinned, her nose crinkling on either side. That smile made her face light up in a way that made his gut jerk even harder. He kicked the sensation away, irritated with himself.

"And you didn't scare me."

He wasn't sure he believed her, but he'd already shown far too much interest in her life—and her—than he should have. The last thing he needed was to have the new nurse get any wrong ideas.

Because there weren't any to have.

And if he was going to get out of here, now was the time to do it without feeling like he'd abandoned her. "Well, I have a few other patients to see, so if you two will excuse me."

"Of course." Nancy sent him a smile,

while Lindy seemed to take her time looking at him, her phone now in her hand, her expression wary once again.

"I'll try to do a little less clock watching the next time we work together." As if she couldn't help herself, her lips soon turned up at the edges and those tiny lines beside her nose reappeared.

He swallowed. "Not a problem. If you have any questions about the hospital or how we do things, I'm sure Nancy, myself or any of the other staff members can steer you in the right direction."

"I appreciate that."

With that he gave the pair a quick wave, before turning around and heading in the opposite direction. Part of him wanted to solve the mystery of the newest staff member and part of him wanted nothing to do with those kinds of guessing games. Especially if it involved someone who'd recently broken up with their spouse or significant other.

Or who had a young daughter.

Better just to do his job and pretend not to notice what Lindy Franklin did or didn't do. As long as she did her job, he had no complaints.

And even if he did, he was going to keep them to himself.

For his own good. And maybe for hers too.

CHAPTER TWO

LINDY WASN'T TOO sure about bringing her mom and Daisy to the hospital for lunch. Especially not after what had happened with Dr....Zeke. Would he think she was distracted again?

She was off duty, so it was really none of his business.

Besides, she hadn't been distracted per se. She'd been well aware of what she was doing and what she was supposed to be doing. And none of that involved the hunky surgeon.

Hunky? Really, Lindy? She gave an internal roll of her eyes.

Besides, her mom wanted to see the hospital, and she could think of no good reason to tell her no. And Daisy had seemed excited about eating somewhere other than at her or Mimi's house.

"It's hospital food, so don't get your hopes up."

Her mom laughed. "I don't have to cook, so I'm sure it'll be great."

"Poor Dad. Is he fending for himself today?"

"No. He's headed to the lodge to see his buddies. Which leaves me with time to spend with my favorite daughter."

"I'm your only daughter, Mom." She flashed a quick smile. "But I'll take whatever time with you I can get."

Especially since she hadn't seen her parents for the duration of her marriage, something that should have sent up a red flag. Luke had supposedly landed a fabulous job across the country almost as soon as the ceremony was over. But, looking back, she wondered if quitting his job in Savannah had been the plan all along. There'd actually been quite a few flags that she'd missed along the way. All because she'd "fallen in love" and hadn't taken precautions. Then, when she'd realized she was pregnant, she'd been too quick to say yes when he'd asked her to marry him.

But no more. If she ever found herself in a relationship again, she was going to make sure she let her mind do most of the work, rather than putting her heart in charge.

She had no desire to jump into that particular lake again. Maybe she'd wait until Daisy was grown up before dating. When she thought about what could have happened the last night she and Luke had been together...

She swallowed, her hand going to her throat as a phantom ache threatened to interfere with her breathing.

Stop it, Lindy. Daisy is fine. You're fine.

Leading the way through the door to the cafeteria, she frowned when she spied the doctor she'd thought of as "hunky" just a few minutes ago. Great. Just what she needed.

She hadn't had to work with him for the last several days, thank God. But she hadn't really expected to see him here either.

Why not? The man had to eat, just like everyone else.

Just as she was ready to shepherd her mom and daughter back the way they'd come with a manufactured excuse, Zeke's eyes met hers, narrowing slightly before moving from her to her mom and then to Daisy.

Then he frowned, deep furrows giving his face an ominous look that made her shiver.

Her chin went up. She wasn't cowering ever again. She had as much of a right to be in here as anyone. She changed her mind about leaving and ushered her mom and Daisy over to the line and got behind them, swinging Daisy up into her arms. "What do you want to eat, honey?"

"Sheeshburger."

"A cheeseburger? How many of those have you had recently?"

Her mom shook her head. "Hey, don't look at me. We had plenty of fruits and vegetables to go with yesterday's burger."

Lindy's dad loved to cook out on the grill, and his meals were always delicious. "I was teasing."

Against her volition, her gaze slid back to Zeke, who she found was still watching her from the coffee bar. The frown was gone, and in its place… Another shiver went through her, this time for a completely different reason. When he snapped the lid onto whatever he'd just poured in his cup, he didn't move away from them like she'd hoped. Instead, he headed their way.

The shivery awareness died a quick death. She had no desire for her daughter to meet any of her male colleagues. Especially not Zeke.

She wanted her daughter to have a good long stretch of stability to hopefully counteract anything she might have seen sensed or heard during her mother's disastrous marriage.

Then Zeke was in line with them. "Hi. You must be off today."

This time it was her brows that came together, until she realized she wasn't dressed in scrubs. Although there were people who did bring their street clothes to work and changed into them after their shift. "I am. I thought I'd show my mom and Daisy around."

"Good idea."

There was an awkward pause, which her mom was quick to fill. "I'm Rachel Anderson. I take it you and my daughter know each other?" She shot Lindy a glance filled with curiosity.

Oh, no, Mom. Not you too.

"He's one of the pediatric surgeons here at the hospital." The words came out a little gruffer than she'd meant for them to.

Zeke held out his hand and introduced himself, making her realize that she should have at least told her mom his name. But the momentary awareness she'd felt a few minutes ago had left her flustered, and Lindy didn't like it. She'd been flustered by Luke as well and look how that had turned out.

"Why don't you join us?" her mom said as Lindy just stood there, staring at him. Damn. Soon Zeke was going to think he'd been right when he'd said she seemed distracted. She was. And this time it wasn't by thoughts of her daughter.

It was by the surgeon himself.

"That's up to Lindy."

What? Why was it up to her? She did not want to cast the deciding vote. "It's fine with me." She shifted Daisy a little higher on her hip, keeping her close. But thankfully Zeke hadn't shown much interest in her daughter. And Lindy would rather keep it that way.

They somehow made it through the line, although she no longer felt like eating. And it wasn't due to the quality of the food on offer in front of them. She tried to take one of the two trays her mom was wrestling with, only to have Zeke take it instead. "I'm not eating much, so I'll put mine on your tray, if that's okay."

Great. She guessed it didn't matter since she'd already said he could join them. "It's fine. No surgeries this afternoon?"

"I had one in the middle of the night and ended up staying. As soon as I eat, I'm heading home to crash."

A surgery in the middle of the night was never a good thing. "Was it bad?"

He nodded, a muscle in his jaw tight. "Very bad. A teenager hung herself."

"Oh, God." Her mom was thankfully ahead of them, since her lungs had suddenly seized as remembered sensations washed over her. The cramping of muscles starved of oxygen. The blackening of her vision.

The realization that if she passed out, it was all over.

Somehow she got hold of herself and swallowed several times to rid herself of the memories. She cleared her throat, somehow needing to ask the question. "Did she make it?"

"Yes. Her trachea suffered a partial separation, and we had to do a tracheotomy and then go in and repair the damage. But she'll be fine physically. And hopefully she'll get the emotional help for whatever caused her to do this."

"How terrible." Lindy had been fortunate that there'd been no permanent damage to her throat. Nothing to repair. Except her heart. And she was still dealing with some of the fallout from that. Like when Nancy had tapped her on the shoulder. Even after two years of freedom, she was sometimes easily startled. And she tended to walk on eggshells around people, afraid of making someone angry, even though she knew that fear was irrational. But, like her therapist had said, it would take time.

Lindy picked out an egg salad sandwich

and a small cup of fruit, while her mom put Daisy's picks on her own tray. And, yes, there was a cheeseburger. That made her smile.

She still had her daughter. There'd been no custody battles. No lengthy court cases. There'd been no need for anything, other than a coffin, in the end. Daisy would never know her father. But she couldn't help but think that was for the best.

A minute or two later they were seated at one of the small tables. Zeke yawned and downed a healthy portion of his coffee.

"Sorry. I'll try not to fall asleep on you."

A pang of compassion went through her. Anyone who saw medicine as a glamorous profession hadn't seen the toll it took on those in the field. Zeke had probably been uprooted from his bed to come in and do the surgery. And then he'd probably gone on rounds this morning and dealt with his own caseload of patients. "Were you scheduled for today?"

"Yes. But I wasn't slated to come in until seven."

"And your surgery was when?"

"Two."

"You have to be exhausted. Are you off tomorrow?" She wasn't sure why she cared. Plenty of healthcare professionals went through the same thing on a daily basis. But she could see the tired lines bracketing his mouth and eyes. Maybe that's what had made his earlier frown seem so fierce.

"Yes."

Her mom laid Daisy's food out on a napkin and put a straw in her cup of juice. "I remember the days when you pulled those kinds of hours before you got…" Her voice faded away.

Thankful her mother had caught herself. Lindy nodded and forced herself to smile. "I'm sure you pulled your share of all-nighters when I was a kid."

"Of course. But that's different from what you and Dr. Bruen do. And you were a pretty healthy child."

As was Daisy, thank goodness.

"Call me Zeke, please."

Lindy's brows went up. So it wasn't just the staff who were allowed to call him by his given name. That privilege evidently extended to their immediate relatives.

He took another gulp of his coffee, bloodshot eyes glancing at her for a second before moving over to Daisy. Then they closed, and he pinched the bridge of his nose as if suddenly sporting a massive headache.

"You don't have to stay here and keep us company. Why don't you go home and get some sleep?" This time her smile wasn't as difficult to find. "Besides, if you drink too much of that stuff you won't be able to do anything but stare at the ceiling."

"Said as if you've done exactly that."

"I have. And it wasn't fun." It also wasn't for the reasons he thought. It had been when her marriage had been at its lowest point, and she'd been worrying about Daisy's future and the hard decision ahead of her. That choice had been taken out of her hands a day later.

At least Daisy would never have to decide whether or not she wanted to see her father in the future.

Zeke pushed his cup away. "I'll take your word for it. And sleep sounds like heaven right now." He stood. "I think I'll try to do just that. Thanks for letting me join you."

"You're welcome."

Daisy lifted her cheeseburger and waved it at him. "Bye-bye."

He looked like he wasn't sure what to do for a second, then he gave a half-smile. "Goodbye to you too. And nice meeting you, Mrs. Anderson."

"Call me Rachel, since I'm calling you Zeke."

"Okay. It was nice meeting you… Rachel."

"You as well."

Once he was gone, her mother looked at her. "The doctors here are a lot cuter than at your last hospital."

"Mom!" It wasn't like she hadn't noticed how good looking Zeke was. The word *hunk*—of all things—wasn't something she threw around every day. But the last thing she needed was to fantasize about the man.

Oh, Lord, no. You are not having fantasies. About anyone!

"Don't you 'Mom' me. You can't let one bad experience turn you off love forever."

"It was a little more than a bad experience, don't you think?" She worded it carefully. Even though Daisy didn't know exactly what had happened, she might be able to understand more than Lindy thought.

"I know, but not all men are like Luke. Take your father, for example."

"I know, but I'm not ready to date. I honestly don't know if I'll ever want to again." Even Mr. Hunk himself would have a hard time moving her off that mark. Even if he wanted to. Which he didn't.

Her mom reached over to squeeze her hand. "I understand. Really, I do. When the time is right, you'll change your mind."

This time Lindy let it go. There was no use arguing over her decisions about dating. And as much as her mom said she understood, how could she possibly know what it had been like to live with someone like Luke? A good chunk of his life insurance policy had gone to pay off credit cards he had taken out in her name. Her discovery of those cards had been what had set him off that last time. It was no wonder she was now leery of relationships. And Daisy had to come first at this point in her life.

"*If* I change my mind, you'll be one of the first to know."

Rachel gave her daughter's hand one last squeeze and then withdrew. "That's my cue to change the subject. Are you getting used to living on your own?"

Lindy's quaint little cottage wasn't all that far from the hospital. It was within walking distance, which was nice. And it overlooked a nearby park, which was even nicer. She and Daisy had strolled through it on more than one occasion already. "I am. Thank you so much for helping me find the house. We're making it a home, little by little, aren't we, Daisy? She loves the princess stickers you got for her wall. We've already put them up."

"Princess!" Daisy said the word in a loud voice.

"I saw them. She is my little princess, aren't you?" Her mom tweaked Daisy's nose.

The tyke repeated the word like a battle cry, stretching her arms out as if showing her grandmother just how much of a princess she was.

They laughed and suddenly Lindy was

fiercely glad she'd decided to return to Savannah when she had. She was back among familiar landmarks and people she loved. It made the odd little pangs in her chest bearable.

She couldn't change the past, but she could make the future something her daughter could look forward to without fear. And if she'd never met Luke, Daisy might not be here at all. Didn't that make it worth it?

Worth it? Lindy hadn't deserved what she'd gotten, but she did love her daughter more than life itself. And, yes, she was glad that at least something good had come out of their marriage.

"I guess I know what she might want to be for Halloween."

Lindy's chest swelled with love. Her mom hadn't showered her with recriminations or accusations. She'd been truly glad that her daughter had come back. If she'd known how the marriage would turn out, she'd kept that declaration to herself. Both of her parents had. They loved Daisy like she did, unconditionally, insisting that they be the ones to provide childcare rather than Lindy finding a daycare center. And Daisy was thriving. Finally. She hadn't noticed the pale fear in her baby's eyes while she'd been in the situation, but now that they were out? Oh, yes, she could see nuances she'd never known were there. It made the guilt that much worse. She'd thought she'd protected Daisy from the worst parts of her marriage, and she had. But, even as an infant, had she been able to pick up on the subtle emotions Lindy thought she'd hidden?

She'd probably never know.

New beginnings.

No more staring in the rearview mirror. There was nothing back there she needed to see. She was supposed to be looking to the future.

And if her glance strayed to places it shouldn't?

Like Zeke Bruen?

Yes. She could acknowledge that he'd caught her eye. But if she was smart, Lindy would make sure that was all he caught: her glance. Because a glance was temporary. A gaze, however…well, that carried a lot more

permanence. And that was going to be re-
served for Daisy and Daisy only.

No matter how difficult that might prove
to be.

Zeke could see Lindy standing by the
nurses' station, staring at the patient board.

Lunch the other day had been a blur of
exhaustion and depleted emotions. Suicide
attempts were always difficult, but this was
one life they'd saved.

For how long, though?

The kicker was that these teens thought
they wanted to die. Zeke's daughter, on the
other hand, had wanted to live. Only she
hadn't gotten to choose.

He glanced at the board. Two of those up
there were his patients. Lindy would be one
of the surgical nurses. He'd asked for her
and wasn't sure why. He suspected some
of it had to do with seeing the object of her
clock-watching up close and personal. Small
and full of smiles, Lindy's daughter was a
miniature version of her. Only Lindy's smile
seemed much more elusive than her child's.
And something Rachel had said stayed with

him over the last couple of days. And he couldn't even remember exactly what it had been. It was more her tone of voice.

He should turn around and walk away before he found himself caught up in something he wanted no part of. But to do so might make her think it was because of her. And she'd be right.

Better that he go over and talk to her as if she were any other member of the team. "Off to an early start?"

She whirled around, a hand pressed to her chest, face draining of all color. When she focused on him, she gave a nervous laugh and leaned back against the counter. "Oh, God, sorry. You startled me."

Startled? That was the second time he'd seen her react like that.

"I didn't mean to. Did you think I was the hospital administrator or something?"

"No." She shook her head. "I was just lost in thought. Didn't anyone ever tell you not to sneak up on people?"

"They did. I just wasn't aware that I was sneaking."

"No, of course you weren't." She sucked

down a deep breath and blew it out. "Sorry. Anyway, did you catch up on your sleep?"

He couldn't remember the last time he'd scared someone like that, and he was pretty sure that time it had been on purpose. But her explanation was reasonable.

"I did, thanks. Just checking in about the surgeries I have scheduled. You'll be scrubbing in on both of them?" Since he'd put her name in as someone he wanted on those cases, the question was more rhetorical than anything.

Her glance went back to the board. "Ledbetter and Brewster? Yes. Anything I should know?"

"Ledbetter has had a reaction to anesthesia before, so they're tweaking the ratios. Just wanted you to be aware in case we have to make a sudden shift in care."

"Okay, got it. And Brewster?"

"We're doing her first. Pneumothorax. Routine."

Lindy gave a visible swallow and looked back up at the board. "She's only five? Since when is a collapsed lung in a child that age considered routine?"

"When that child has been kicked by her father. And I worded that badly. It's never routine." Just saying the words made a jet of anger spurt through Zeke's chest. What kind of monster hurt his own child? Or any child?

"That's horrible." Her voice came out as a whisper.

The boards listed names and ages and team members, but nothing more.

"I know. I thought maybe you'd looked at the charts."

She reached behind her and gripped the edge of the desk. "I just got here. I was going to look at them once I figured out which cases I'd be working on."

The hospital had code numbers for staffing the surgical suites, with the surgeons sometimes handpicking their crews, and other times it was the luck of the draw, depending on scheduling.

Zeke had asked for her, telling himself he wanted to see her in action now that he knew a little more about her. There were a few surgical nurses that he preferred not to work with, either because they were difficult or because they were slow to hand over instruments. Every surgeon had their own style and not everyone meshed with his. He knew he could sometimes be demanding.

Like confronting Lindy about being distracted that first time working together?

It had nothing to do with idle interest and everything to do with watching her work. She definitely had compassion, judging from her reaction to the patient with the collapsed lung.

"These kinds of cases are always difficult."

"Yes. Yes, they are."

The thread of resignation in her voice gave him pause. Maybe her other hospital saw more cases involving domestic violence than Mid Savannah did, although even one case was too many.

"We'll get her patched up, and hopefully the system will do what it's supposed to do and keep her out of that home. I think the dad is in jail right now."

"As well he should be. And her mother?"

"She said she was at work when the incident happened."

"The incident. That's one way to put it."

Her tight voice spoke volumes. Then she sighed. "Sorry. I didn't mean to snap. The wheels of justice just never seem to turn fast enough."

"I didn't think you were, and you're right, they don't. But those wheels can't move on their own. There has to be that initial push."

First she'd jumped when he'd come up behind her, now this. Was she just out of sorts today or was something else going on?

"Those situations are just so hard. I actually volunteered at a center helping victims of domestic violence, so it's just straying a bit too close to home."

"That's interesting. I sat in on a meeting of department heads a couple of weeks ago. The hospital has discussed putting together a center for victims of domestic violence or abuse. They already have a grant from a private donor, but they need someone to jump start things. So far no one has stepped up to volunteer."

Lindy's head came up. "Really? I would love to be involved."

"Are you still volunteering somewhere?"

"Not at the moment. I took a leave of absence so I could focus on this job. I thought once I got established I could go back at some point."

An alarm sounded in one of the rooms and a light flashed in the panel of monitors behind her. She glanced back.

"Go," he said. "I'll see you in surgery as soon as our patient is prepped. If you're serious about helping out with the center, let the administrator know. I'm sure they could use someone who already knows the ropes."

"Thanks. I might just do that." With that, she walked away, headed for the nearby room, leaving Zeke with more questions than answers. He was usually pretty adept at figuring people out after talking with them a time or two. But she was proving to be an enigma.

There was part of him, though, that wondered if he wasn't missing something obvious.

Like what?

He had no idea. And he was definitely not going to start asking her a bunch of questions. He barely knew her. Maybe he should drop in on the hospital administrator himself and let the cat out of the bag about her experience. Not everyone could stomach what went on behind closed doors. The fact that she could…

How did one decide to volunteer for something like that? Especially if you had no first-hand knowledge?

Something kicked up in the back of his head. Lindy had never mentioned a husband.

So? That meant nothing.

Or did it?

Back at the cafeteria it had been Daisy and her mother with no mention of anyone else being involved in her life.

Again, it might not be significant.

And if it was?

Then helping with the program might be the best thing that Lindy could do. Not only for the hospital's sake. But if the weird feelings he had going on were true, then it might do Lindy some good as well.

CHAPTER THREE

FIVE DAYS AFTER helping to re-inflate a little girl's damaged lung, Lindy went and talked to the administrator about the program and offered to help. In doing so, she told him about her past, including the truth behind Luke's death. As she did so, a weight lifted off her chest. He asked if she'd be willing to speak at an informal Q&A about the program that was already in the works. If there was interest, they would move forward. If not, they wouldn't. He would leave it up to her as far as how much she shared.

Could she do it? Well, it was too late now, since she'd already agreed. She just had to figure out what she was going to say.

By concealing her past from her colleagues, she'd wondered if she wasn't contributing to a culture that encouraged people to hide behind a mask of normalcy.

In fact, she'd almost told Zeke in front of the schedule board as they'd talked about the little girl's injuries but had chickened out. If he was at the meeting, he would probably soon know, anyway. And that scared her to death. Would he look at her differently? Feel pity for her?

She didn't know why it mattered, but it did.

As painful as it was to look back at what had happened, Zeke's words about the wheels needing a push to start them turning made a lot of sense. In fact, they'd played over and over in her head all weekend long, and they were still going strong today. Even if it was just manning a phone on a helpline for an hour or two a week after her shift, she could help to be that push that changed someone's life for the better. And it fit right in with her "new beginnings" motto.

She might not be a trained psychologist, but she was a medical professional. She also had first-hand knowledge of the excuses that kept someone from leaving a deplorable relationship. She'd used those same excuses. Luke's gambling problems—which she hadn't known about when they'd dated—had been spiraling out of control for years.

That was probably part of the reason for the job change right after their marriage, although she didn't know that for sure. He'd gone to great lengths to hide the truth, his behavior becoming more and more erratic and threatening. Once she'd found out about the credit cards he'd taken out in her name, it was all over. Lindy had almost lost her life. But in the end, it was Luke who'd paid the ultimate price.

She still had nightmares about the last day they'd been together. In fact, the night before Zeke had startled her, she'd woken up in a cold sweat and had lain awake for hours. So when Zeke's voice had come out of nowhere at the desk that day, her hands had curled into fists out of instinct.

There'd been no danger, though. Not from him.

But it also made her aware of how she'd changed in the years since the police had come to arrest her husband. She'd dropped her guard in some ways, but in other ways those walls were just as tall and as thick as they'd ever been. Time did dull the fear, but it hadn't obliterated it completely.

And maybe that was a good thing. It kept her wary of what could happen if she didn't stay vigilant. She'd made a vow to herself never to put her daughter in a situation like that again.

Would Zeke be interested in volunteering, if the hospital program did get underway?

What had even brought that to mind?

Maybe the memory of the way he'd operated on five-year-old Meredith Brewster. That man had been a study in compassion that brought tears to her eyes. He'd been worried about an injury to her spleen. Something that was insidious, often having few symptoms as the organ slowly filled with blood. But if it ruptured, the effects could be catastrophic. Luckily everything had come back normal, aside from the collapsed lung and a fractured rib.

Normal?

Nothing about it had been normal.

But she could be the change that started

that wheel turning. And maybe asking Zeke to help could be part of that initial push.

Besides, she was curious about what his response would be.

She was sure her parents wouldn't mind watching Daisy for an hour while she talked to the group. Even if it meant exposing scars that weren't completely healed?

If not now, then when?

That was the question and one she had no answer to. So it was time to jump in and make sure that terrible period in her life did some good. Even if it meant she and Zeke might be seeing a lot more of each other.

She wasn't watching the clock. It appeared Lindy had been able to settle into her role of surgical nurse without worrying about her daughter.

Not much of her face was visible with the mask and surgical cap. But those light brown eyes were there. And they were still wreaking havoc with his insides. They came up unexpectedly and caught him looking. Damn. He needed to pay more attention to

what he was about to do and less attention
to the way she was affecting him.

This might be a routine 'scope, but the
child deserved every ounce of his attention.
He jerked his glance to the anesthesiologist,
who was standing at her head. "She's ready
for the procedure," the man said.

The twilight sedation would allow his patient to swallow and follow instructions, but
she would have little or no memory of doing
so when they were done with the procedure.

Zeke pulled the loupes down over his
eyes. "Okay, Tessa, open your mouth."

It always amazed him that part of the
brain was still aware and could obey simple commands even while the patient's con-
scious self was wandering through a gray
haze. He slid the endoscope into place. "Big
swallow."

Tessa complied, gagging slightly as the
scope was introduced. Then it was all business.

"Suction."

Lindy was right there, clearing excess
moisture from the child's mouth.

He relayed his observations, knowing

the microphone that hung overhead would pick up his words, which he could transcribe later. "Pink mucosa with no abnormalities. Advancing to the sphincter."

He then slid past it, moving into the main part of Tessa's stomach. This was where he needed to take his time. "How's the patient doing, Steve?"

"Everything looks good."

He adjusted the focus of the 'scope and went over the surface of the stomach. "Normal appearance of the fundus and the lesser curvature." But when he turned the 'scope to face the other direction he pulled up short. There was a large eroded section of the lining and a mass about the size of a golf ball. "I'm seeing a nodule with irregular borders in the middle of the greater curvature. There is a moderate amount of erosion of the surrounding tissue. Going to attempt a biopsy of the mass."

He moved in closer and changed the setting, snapping several pictures, and then grabbed a piece of the tissue with the pincers. He cut and cauterized in one fluid motion. "I've got it. Bleeding is negligible."

He surveyed the rest of the stomach but didn't see anything else abnormal, so he eased the 'scope out, his chest tight. He had only seen one other growth similar to this one and the outcome hadn't been good. He could only hope the pathology findings were different in this case and would allow the child to go on with her life.

This time it was Lindy's eyes who were on him, the narrow furrow between her brows saying that she'd had the same suspicion. But now wasn't the time to dwell on that. He needed to finish the procedure and make sure Tessa was okay. Then they could worry about the other stuff.

Fifteen minutes later, she was waking up, lids fluttering as her awareness returned. "Am I okay?" Her voice was raspy, which was normal.

"You did just fine." It wasn't exactly what she'd asked, but close enough. He forced a smile, pulling down his mask so she could see his face. "That wasn't so bad, was it?"

But what was coming might very well prove to be.

"No, I didn't feel anything."

"That's what I like to hear. Dr. Black is pretty good at his job." He glanced at Steve, whose face was as solemn as everyone else's.

"I do my best." The other doctor laid his hand on her head, ignoring the surgical cap. "You did a good job too, kiddo."

Yes, she had. And she'd been stoic every time he'd met with her parents, although they described her pain levels as varying between moderate and debilitating. And now he had to go out and talk to them. The procedure itself had gone like clockwork. Everything else? Well, they would know that soon enough.

"I'm going to go see your mom and dad and let them know you're awake, okay? They'll be able to see you once we get you into your room."

He motioned for Lindy to follow him out. "You said you wanted to talk to me?" She'd mentioned wanting to meet with him after the procedure.

"It can wait."

He frowned at her. Maybe it could, but with the way his day had been he might not have many opportunities to come find her later on. "Follow me down to the waiting room. We can discuss whatever it is afterward."

"Seriously, it's nothing important. Not like…" Her voice trailed away, but he knew what she meant.

"Maybe not, but I think I need something else to think about once this is over."

"It's a hard case."

"Yes, it is." She had no idea how hard. And he hadn't been joking when he'd said he needed something else to think about. Cases like Tessa's brought back memories that were still raw and painful, even after five years. He remembered all too well the pain of that diagnosis, of the symptoms he felt he should have seen. Of the fear that had followed him all the way down to the bitter end.

Did Lindy ever wonder about Daisy when she went into that operating room? Did she think about what it would be like to…lose her? He swallowed hard to control his emotions, forcing himself back to the here and now.

Heading toward the waiting room, Lindy

took out her phone and trailed behind a few steps. Texting to see how her daughter was? If it had been him, that's exactly what he would have been doing. Instead, he was pushing through the door to the waiting room to address two people who still had their daughter.

For now, at least.

"Mr. and Mrs. Williams?" He turned his thoughts to his patient's care. The family deserved that.

Tessa's mom and dad separated themselves from a group of people who had been huddled in the back. Zeke was glad he'd stripped his surgical gown and cap off, although he wasn't sure why. He normally left them on, choosing to notify the family as soon as possible. But he'd wanted to face them as a human being first and a doctor second.

Mr. Williams clasped his wife's hands in his. "How is she?"

"The procedure went very well. Tessa is already awake and will be anxious to see you, although her throat will be sore, and she may still be a little bit groggy." He paused. "Can we sit for a minute?"

He motioned to a bank of chairs that were a little removed from the group, sensing they would rather hear the details in private. He glanced at Lindy and gave a slight nod to indicate that she was welcome to join them. He hoped she did, in fact. "This is Lindy Franklin, she's a surgical nurse who assisted me."

"Tessa is a very sweet girl," Lindy said.

Mrs. Williams already had tears streaming down her face, maybe sensing what was to come. "Do either of you have children?"

Zeke froze, the way he did every time he was asked that question. What did he say? Yes, he had a child? Because saying he'd had a daughter who had died of an insidious disease would do nothing to help reassure the two people in front of him.

Lindy saved him from having to say anything. "I have a little girl. She's three. Her name is Daisy."

Tessa's mom nodded and then turned her gaze to him. "It's bad, isn't it?"

"We did find a mass in her stomach. We biopsied it but won't know exactly what we're dealing with until the pathology results come back."

Mr. Williams put his arm around his wife's shoulders. "What do you *think* it is?"

"I don't really want to speculate. It could be benign." He leaned forward, planting his elbows on his knees. "Let's just take this one step at a time, shall we?"

Tessa's father dragged a hand through his hair, his eyes closing for a second. Then he looked at Zeke with a steady gaze. Steadier than Zeke's had been when he'd heard a piece of devastating news. "How long before the results are back?"

"I'm thinking they should be in by Monday. I'll call you as soon as we hear anything."

Mr. Williams drew his wife closer as tears silently tracked down her face. "Thank you for everything." He glanced at Lindy. "And you as well."

"I was happy to be there." The sincerity in her voice was unmistakable. A zip of pride went through him at the great team they had at Mid Savannah. And that included Lindy. Two weeks ago he hadn't even been sure he was going to like her, and now he was sitting here glad she'd come with him to notify the parents. Glad that she'd worked beside him in that operating room. There was something about her that…

Maybe it was the fact that she had a child almost the same age as his would have been. His eyes skimmed down her profile as she quietly talked to Mrs. Williams about the joys of having a daughter.

He'd once known that same joy.

But there were joys in the memories, weren't there?

Yes, but not enough to want to go on that particular journey again. He'd seen enough in his days as a doctor to make him realize how very tenuous life was and all the things that could go wrong. He saw it day in and day out. Even sitting here talking to Tessa's parents. He had no idea what they were facing.

And Zeke wasn't sure he could face those kinds of odds again in his own life.

As glad as he was to have Lindy here for moral support, he'd better make sure it stayed on a professional footing. Having lunch with her mom and daughter last week had been harder than he'd thought it would be. He dealt with kids every day, but for the most part he was able to compartmentalize that. But interacting on a social level was something else entirely. By the end of the meal, he'd found himself avoiding the child's glance in order to make it through until the end. Hopefully he'd hidden it well enough that they hadn't guessed.

They finished up their conversation and the parents looked at him as if waiting for him to make another statement. "You're welcome to go see her now. And as soon as the discharge papers are ready, you can take her home." He forced a smile. "I'm sure she's more than ready. You'll be hearing from us early next week."

They thanked him again and headed over to be with their family. Tessa's mom was immediately caught up in the embrace of an older woman. Her mother, maybe? He was glad this family could support each other through the good times and the not so good—something he hadn't had.

Lindy met him outside the doors. "Are you okay?" she asked.

"Fine." He leaned against the wall and faced her. Had she seen something in his expression back there? Hell, he hoped not. "Now, what was it you wanted to say to me?"

He hadn't meant it to sound brusque, but when her eyes flickered and glanced away he realized the rough edge hadn't gone unnoticed. Dammit, why did he always do this? He'd done it with Janice too, pushing her away when they should have been clinging to each other.

Turning toward her, he let his fingers trail over hers in apology. The warmth of her skin, even with that brief contact, awoke an answering warmth within him that quickly spread. Big mistake. Big honking mistake.

"Sorry, Lindy. It's been a long, hard day."

"I know, and I don't mean to add to it. Like I said, it can wait."

The warmth evaporated, a sudden chill sending prickles over his scalp. A thought hit him, and his gut lurched sideways. "Are you quitting?"

"What? No." She wore scrubs adorned in balloons today, the multicolored bunches that danced across her red top looking almost obscenely cheerful after the procedure they'd just taken part in. Worse was the fact that his touch hadn't seemed to hijack her senses the way it had his. Except, when he looked closer, her pupils were large and bottomless, handing back his reflection in a way that made him wonder.

She bit her lip. And, dammit, that act sent his thoughts careening in a completely different direction.

"You don't *want* me to quit, do you?" she asked.

He forced his eyes back up. No. He didn't. And he wasn't sure how he felt about that.

"No, of course not. You handled things with Tessa's parents admirably. Better than I did, actually."

She grinned, looking relieved. "Doctors don't always have the best reputation as far as that goes."

Thankful for the lighter tone, he feigned offense. "We don't?"

This time she laughed. "You know you don't."

"Well, on that note, let's change the subject to something a bit more positive."

"Okay, so I did something." She reached into the pocket of her scrubs and pulled out a sheet of printer paper with something typed on it. "I took your advice and went to see the hospital administrator."

He focused on her words, not quite sure what they meant for a second. Then his gaze shifted to the sheet, more notably the hand holding it. It was shaking.

So much for a lighter tone. He started to ask about it, but a group of residents walked by, laughing about something one of them had done earlier today.

"Let's go back to my office. We can talk there."

They arrived, and Lindy dropped into one of the leather chairs.

He rounded the desk and sat as well. "You talked to the hospital administrator about…" Their earlier conversation came flooding back. "About the women's crisis center?"

"Yes."

"What did he say?"

"Well, I remembered what you said about a wheel needing a push to get it turning—"

"I said that?"

She leaned forward in her chair, seeming more at ease now. "You did, actually. And so I went in and gave a little push. I volunteered to help with it."

That shocked him. He hadn't really expected her to go in, even though he'd been the one to suggest it. Or that his words had been what had spurred her to action. He wasn't sure whether to feel guilty or glad.

"And?"

"He's planning on having an informal Q&A on Friday. And he wants me to do one of the presentations."

Lindy? He knew she'd volunteered for a period of time, but it almost sounded like she'd done more than that. "Wow. That's great. What are you presenting?"

"About why the community needs something like this so much."

"It does, of course." He still wasn't quite sure what was happening. "The hard part seems to be getting women in those situations to leave…to get away from the person or situation."

"I know." She shook her head before he had a chance to say anything else. "No, Zeke. I *really* know."

The emphasis on that word made him stare. "Oh, hell, Lindy. You?"

"Yes, unfortunately. That's what Neil wants me to talk about. I was one of the ones who stayed. Until I realized it wasn't just about me anymore. It was also about my daughter."

His jaw tightened until it sent a warning. He would never understand it. What kind of man hurt the people he was supposed to love?

Well, he might as well point that finger back at himself. Hadn't he hurt Janice by refusing to acknowledge her requests to talk? By not budging when she asked him to redirect his professional life to something that didn't involve kids? But he'd never in a million years raised a hand to her or any other woman.

It didn't make any sense to him. And what kind of person stayed?

Lindy had, evidently. An ache settled in his chest.

"And if Daisy hadn't come along?" The thought of her cowering in a corner while some piece of scum stood over her, glorying in what he'd made her do, made Zeke want to do some serious damage to the man.

"I think I eventually would have left. At least I hope I would have."

The ache spread to the backs of his eyes.

"Is he in prison?"

"No."

Shock roiled through him. Had she not pressed charges?

"He's still out there? They didn't prosecute?"

"He's not out there."

"But I thought you said—"

"I did." She shut her eyes for a second before fixing him with a look that made his blood run cold. "He's dead. And before you ask, no, I didn't pull the trigger. The police did."

He hadn't expected that. Then again, he hadn't expected Lindy to just admit that she'd once been one of those that Mid Savannah hoped to help.

"God. I'm sorry."

"Don't be. The only people I'm sorry for is his family. His parents had no idea what was going on. And I said nothing. I know exactly what it's like to cake on makeup and present a smiling face to hide the damage."

"How long were you with him?"

"A year. I left him two years ago."

Daisy would have been, what, one at the time? Hopefully too young to remember anything.

"I'll say it again… I'm sorry. Not that he's dead, but that you went through any of it."

"I wish I'd left sooner. But there came a point when I didn't have a choice. When I realized that if I didn't get out right then, I probably wasn't going to live to see another day."

She'd almost died? Hell, what had the man done to her?

He reached across and put his hand over the one holding the flyer. "I'm glad."

"You're glad…?"

"That you left."

"So am I. The kicker is that he died before I could get a divorce. So according to legal documents I'm a widow, not a divorcee."

The irony wasn't lost on him.

"At least he's out of your life."

"Not entirely, I'm afraid. Luke had a gambling problem. Some of the debts he incurred affected my credit, even though I paid them off."

This was one of the things that people didn't think of: the financial ramifications of leaving and how to navigate those waters. No wonder Neil wanted her to speak.

"Did you see an attorney?"

"Yep. He helped me negotiate with the credit bureaus to wipe out some of the ones Luke defaulted on. But I couldn't prove that all of them were his."

"Do you need help?"

"What?" Her eyes widened, then flashed with anger. "No. I can manage just fine on my own."

Realizing he'd offended her, he rephrased slightly. "I didn't mean to imply that you couldn't. Sorry if it sounded that way."

"It's okay." She smiled. "Maybe I haven't

come as far as I thought I had. I still get defensive from time to time. And having people come up behind me can still make me jumpy."

He'd witnessed that a couple of times. He let go of her hand and came around the front of the desk, sitting on the edge of it. "That's why you took a few years off. It wasn't just because of Daisy."

Another thing that was none of his business. But he was curious.

"Yes. He didn't want me to work…wanted me there when he got home. At first I convinced myself that it was sweet, and that I would be perfectly happy as a housewife and mother. Lots of women are, and I think that's their path. But I have always enjoyed my job. I'm glad to be back in the thick of it."

"Well, we're happy to have you."

This made her laugh. "Are you? That's quite a turnaround from my first day on the job."

An extra little cleft appeared in her left cheek when she smiled. Not a dimple exactly but more of a line caused by her smile pulling more to one side than the other. Whatever it was, it was damned attractive. As was that glossy head of dark hair.

Easy, Bruen. You don't need to be noticing things like that. Especially not on someone who's suffered so much hurt at the hands of another man.

Maybe his reaction was just a misplaced sense of needing to protect someone.

Whatever it was, he was glad she'd landed at Mid Savannah Medical Center.

"I guess it is a little bit of a turnaround." And he wasn't exactly sure what had made the difference. Maybe it was that smile. Or maybe it had nothing to do with the ridiculous way he seemed to be noticing everything about her. Much better to attribute it to the dedication he saw in her after that first wobbly start.

And he couldn't fault her for worrying or staring at the clock that day.

Weren't there days when his lungs still slammed shut in grief over a loss he might have been able to prevent had he recognized the signs? Yes, there were. More of them than he cared to admit.

It was strange how death could be at opposite ends of the spectrum. To one person, it meant freedom from abuse. To another, it meant the loss of something irretrievable and precious. Like his daughter. And the trust of his ex-wife.

"So this is my cue to ask you that question I mentioned."

"Question? I thought you wanted to tell me that you went to the hospital administrator."

"Yes, that, but I also wanted to see if you'd be interested in volunteering."

His eyes widened. "You want *me* to volunteer? In the program? I thought that's what I was asking you to do?"

"You did. And I am. But you're the head of pediatric surgery. You can bring another side to this. There are a lot of women who were in the same position I was. Women with children. Women who stay, in spite of those children." He watched her take a deep breath. "Remember Meredith Brewster?"

"The pneumothorax case?"

"Yes. There are thousands of Meredith Brewsters out there, who get hurt because women stayed in terrible relationships. You could speak about that. Tell hurting women what you've seen over the years. Maybe you can change someone's mind."

He frowned. "I'm not sure about that. Would I have changed your mind?"

The answer was suddenly very important to him. Especially in light of what he'd just learned about her.

Her eyes met his, staring at him for a long second. "Yes. I think you might have." Her index finger wrapped around his. "This feels right, Zeke. I'm glad I'm here."

Glad she was at Mid Savannah? Or glad she was in his office, practically holding his hand?

Because hell if he wasn't glad of both of those things.

The swirling in his head started again, maybe in reaction to her words. Or the light scent that her movements sent his way. Whatever it was, it was making him want to do something crazy. Something more than what they were currently doing.

"I'm glad you are too." He turned his palm and caught her hand, drawing her to her feet. "And it does feel right. Very, very right."

Her eyes held his, a growing warmth in their depths he hadn't noticed when this conversation had started.

He tightened his grip slightly and the muscles in his biceps tightened as he drew her hand closer. Except it wasn't just her hand that answered the request. Her whole body did, taking a step toward him.

Sliding off his desk, he found himself standing within inches of her. He willed himself to let go of her, and he succeeded in uncurling his fingers. Except his hand seemed to have a mind of its own, lifting to cup her face.

"Yes. I think you could have talked me into almost anything."

As soon as she said the words he was lost, his mouth coming down to meet hers and finding her lips so much softer than he expected. And when she kissed him back, his world exploded—a million fragments flying in all directions. And for once in his life he didn't care which pieces he found. Or which ones were lost forever.

CHAPTER FOUR

SHE'D THOUGHT SHE'D never enjoy another kiss.

But, God, when Zeke asked if he could have made her change her mind, she'd melted inside. He acted like it mattered. Said that her being here did feel right.

And so did this.

The heady warmth of his mouth filled her senses, and she couldn't get enough of the taste of him, of the smooth slide of skin against skin. It all melded together into a luscious blend she would never get out of her head. The second he'd come around that desk, she'd started wondering what it would be like if he touched her.

It was so much better than she imagined.

Maybe that was what had made her curl her finger around his. Curiosity. What she hadn't expected was the jolt of need that rocked her world and nearly made her gasp aloud. Had she ever experienced that before? She didn't think so.

Then he'd done the unthinkable and wrapped his whole hand around hers. Her senses had been swamped. A tsunami striking shore and wiping out every rational thought in its path.

She was still caught in its grip.

A tiny sound came out of her throat, and she inched closer, his hard chest brushing her breasts. Her nipples tightened instantly.

She wanted him with everything that she had.

The hands that had been cupping her face moved to her hips, and she thought he was going to haul her against him completely, but he didn't. His grip was tight, but it was as if he were holding her in place, keeping her still. Was he trying to torture her?

Something warred inside her, telling her to take another step and test that theory… see just how strong his resolve was, and just how much this kiss was affecting him.

Surely he'd been swept along by the same wave.

I dare you, Lindy. Do it.

She opened her mouth, dumbfounded by the fact that it was something she'd never done before. Would never have thought of doing.

Ever.

The thought awoke some rational part of her brain, and she froze.

What was she doing here? Wasn't this exactly what she'd warned herself about: impulsively jumping into something she should avoid?

Maybe. But for now…

She closed her eyes, realizing this was about to end. Just one more second. Then she would move away.

As if he'd read her thoughts, the pressure on her hips increased. Only instead of easing her closer, he propelled her a step backward, removing all points of contact—right before his head lifted.

There was a glazed look in his eyes, that said stopping hadn't been easy.

Well, join the club, mister.

Only in the end he'd been stronger than she had, and that bothered her on a level she didn't want to explore.

He spoke up first. "Damn." He pulled in

an audible breath and let it hiss back out. "I'm sorry, Lindy. I have no idea where that came from."

She did, but she wasn't about to shoulder the blame by herself. At least not out loud. Inside, it was a whole different matter. She was the one who'd started down this road, but she wasn't quite sure why. Maybe the realization that she wasn't afraid of him, at least not physically.

Emotionally?

Lord. This man could destroy her, if she let him.

She needed to make sure something like this didn't happen again. She'd been so proud of her resolve, telling herself she would turn down any and all offers to date if they came about, which they hadn't.

Would I have changed your mind?

His earlier words whispered through her head, and suddenly she wasn't sure she could have been as strong as she'd thought. If he'd asked her out, could she have refused?

Hadn't that kiss answered that question? It had.

And that scared her on a completely different level.

She went with the first thing that came to mind. "Domestic violence is an emotional subject. You didn't know about my past—and, honestly, I had no intention of saying anything until the Q&A. The last thing I need is anyone's pity."

Oh, God, was that why he'd kissed her? Because he felt sorry for her?

"You think that came out of pity?"

This time he took hold of her hips and tugged her against him, making her very aware of where things stood between them. "This has nothing to do with pity."

Then he was gone, this time back behind the refuge of his desk, leaving her standing there…her breathing not completely normal yet. Neither was the rest of her. Little charges of electricity were still zapping between neurons, hoping to be reignited.

Not a chance.

She needed to get out of there. Before she did something she'd regret.

"I should go."

He pushed the flyer across the desk to her.

"If you still want me to be there on Friday, I will. How long does my part of the presentation have to be?"

She was tempted to tell him to stay away. But surely by the end of the week she'd be able to put out the rest of today's embers.

And if she couldn't?

Then she was in big trouble.

"Around ten minutes. Do you want me to put you down?"

His thumb tapped out a rhythm on the surface of his desk, and she held her breath. As scary as this was, she really did think he could make a difference in the program.

And if he ended up making a difference in her instead?

Well, she would have to deal with that when and if it came up.

"Yes. Put me down."

"Okay, I will. And thank you."

She didn't say what she was thanking him for. Instead, she just turned around and hightailed it out of there, all the while praying that tomorrow would find her strong enough to put this all behind her.

Because the last thing she needed was to

get involved with someone, especially someone she worked with. Because if things went
south…

*Lindy, they've already gone so far south
they've jumped off the bottom of the globe.*

Ha! Well, then, it was up to her to reel
them back in until her feet were standing
on firm ground.

No more talk of tsunamis. Or electrical
charges.

And, most of all, no more kissing of
hunky surgeons.

Who was she kidding? The truth was she
would probably be reliving that kiss in her
dreams. Tonight. Tomorrow night. And any
number of unnamed nights in the future.

And although Friday might seem like
quite a way off right now, it would come
long before she was ready for it to.

So all she could do was regroup, and hope
she could pretend she'd recovered from their
encounter. Even if it was a complete and
utter lie.

Tessa's results were in. Zeke counted to five
before opening the digital file. Either her

parents would be referred to an oncologist, or he would schedule her for surgery to remove a benign tumor. He certainly knew what he hoped for. But what he hoped for didn't always come to pass.

He clicked on the folder, his glance skipping through everything but the meat of the report: *...atypical cells...noninvasive...*

He almost went slack with relief. It wasn't quite benign, but it wasn't cancerous either and more than likely confined to the area in which it was found. That was good news. Great news, in fact.

The tumor would still have to be removed, and Zeke would need to get clean margins so that the growth didn't come back, but there would be no need for radiation or chemo treatments.

His fingers went to his cellphone to tell Lindy the good news, then he stopped. He didn't usually call his surgical team individually and relay test results. They normally found out, but that was because of followup surgery or treatment.

The truth was he just wanted to hear her voice. Maybe to make sure she was okay.

His oath as a doctor was to do no harm. And he wasn't quite sure he'd lived up to that in this case.

He still wasn't sure what had caused that kiss the other day, even though he had repeatedly micro-analyzed everything that had led up to it. To the point that it kept him awake at night and had ended with him standing under a cold blast of water on one occasion.

Not that he was any closer to an answer now than he had been the day it happened. It had changed the way he scheduled his surgeries, though. Whereas where he might have requested her as part of his team before, he was now loath to attach her name to anything connected with him. She'd probably noticed, but if she was smart, she'd be relieved by it.

Of course, there was the little matter of her wanting him to help with the Q&A on Friday and with the program itself, but surely that wouldn't require a lot of time together.

He picked up the phone again. But this time it was because he remembered her asking to be kept in the loop regarding Tessa's results. But maybe he would simply text her rather than call.

He punched in the words as quickly as he could, as if it would limit his contact with her. Tessa's results are in. Atypical cells, but no malignancy. Will follow up with surgery at a later date. He then hit "send" and set the phone down again, forcing himself to go back to work, rather than worry about whether or not she would get the message and/or respond. He'd almost succeeded when a little *ding* told him he had an incoming message.

From Lindy?

Just leave it.

Too late. His glance was already on the screen. It was from Lindy, but the message was short and succinct. So glad!

And that was that.

The next thing he knew, the phone was ringing. He swallowed when he saw it was from the same person.

This time his subconscious didn't argue with him. He picked it up and punched the button. "Bruen here."

As if she wouldn't know who was on the line.

"Hi, um… I was just checking to see if you know when surgery will be."

"I haven't scheduled it yet. I just got the report."

"Oh, okay." She hesitated, then said, "I'd like to be on the surgical team, if I could."

"Of course." He wasn't sure why she felt she had to ask. His heart clenched. Maybe because he'd avoided putting her on the schedule. It had probably made something that wasn't really a big deal into something more than it was. Except to him it had been a very big deal. He'd never kissed a woman in his office before. And certainly not someone he worked with.

"I was already planning on it."

"It just seemed as if…"

He could almost hear the shrug on the other end of the line. Not willing to confirm that he was avoiding her, he countered by finishing her sentence in a completely different way. "It just seemed as if the schedules have changed? They have. I feel like I've been overtaxing some of the nurses and am trying to make things a little more equitable. Spread the load out among more people."

It wasn't exactly the truth, but it was better than saying he didn't want to work with her anymore. Because he did. He just wasn't sure it was a good idea.

"Okay. I just didn't want what happened to change our working relationship."

He assumed she was speaking somewhere where she couldn't be overheard. Maybe she wasn't even at the hospital today. "It won't as long as neither of us lets it."

Hadn't he already done that?

"Thank you. I, um… I promise I wasn't throwing myself at you."

That was the last thing he would expect from her. "I know. I promise I wasn't throwing myself at you either." He couldn't stop the smile that formed at those words. "Like you said, Lindy, it was an emotional subject. I think it just caught us both off guard. I'm glad you told me, though. I do think you'll be a great asset to the new program."

"I think you will be as well. You still want to come, don't you?"

Hmm…that was probably going to be a yes on more than one level. But he wasn't going there.

"I do. And like I said, you're the perfect person to talk about what it's like to survive domestic violence. Not everyone there has been through what you have."

"I'm very glad of that." He thought he heard a sigh. "I'd appreciate it if you'd keep this between the two of us."

Was she talking about the kiss or her background? It didn't matter. He'd never been one for indulging in workplace gossip—or workplace romances, for that matter—and he wasn't about to start now. "Don't worry about it. I've told no one. It's no one's business but yours."

"Thank you. I know I'm talking about it at the meeting, but I'd rather control how much is shared."

"Completely understandable." He picked up a pencil and wiggled it between his fingers, surprised by how comfortable he felt talking to her, even after what had happened. What he'd expected had been awkward silences on both ends of the line. It was nice. As was hearing her voice again.

A little too nice.

"Well, I'll let you go."

The pencil went still. "Okay. I'll let you know when Tessa's surgery is."

They said their goodbyes and then she was gone, leaving him to wonder if the next face-to-face meeting would prove to be just as easy as that phone conversation had been.

Somehow, he doubted it. But if they could do it once, they could do it again. At least he hoped so. Because it would make work—and his life—that much easier.

Why had he thought this would be easy? He scheduled Lindy on his next surgical day and the second he saw her brown eyes peering at him from above that mask, he knew he should have waited a few more days. Because his glance had slid over her and remembered exactly what her lips looked like. What they felt like.

How they tasted.

Damn. But the only thing he could do was

stick to the plan of getting past that memory. It would get easier with time.

Lindy, on the other hand, seemed fine. Her eyes twinkled when she saw him, and he knew she was smiling beneath the mask, her nose crinkling in that adorable way that went straight to his gut. "This looks like an interesting case."

It was going to be interesting all right. And that wasn't including the case.

"The infection hasn't responded to antibiotics, like we'd hoped." These pulmonary cases actually were interesting, but they were also nerve-racking. There was always the possibility of spreading the bacteria to other parts of the lung. This time, though, the pocket of infection was encapsulated and hopefully it could be removed and the lung re-sectioned, barring any complications.

That wasn't the only reason they were nerve-racking. They also brought up a lot of unwanted memories. His ex-wife had wanted him to change specialties for just this reason. Pulmonary cases almost always sent him home in a stupor that had nothing to do with drugs or alcohol.

That first year had been the worst. He would spend weeks either not speaking or lashing out in anger if Janice tried to talk to him. Not physically, but he'd made it clear he didn't want to interact. In failing his daughter, he'd also failed his wife. She'd needed him. And he hadn't been there. She'd rightfully filed for divorce on the anniversary of Marina's death.

"Zeke?"

Lindy had asked him a question.

"Sorry, what?"

"How many of these have you done?"

He told the truth. "Too many." He'd saved a lot of lives, but he'd also lost the one he'd needed to save the most.

His daughter had died of childhood interstitial lung disease, only he hadn't recognized it for what it was. Not at first. Not until it had been far too late.

The guilt of that had almost killed him. He was a surgeon, supposedly one of the top in his field, and still he'd missed it.

He could remember the times when Marina's cough had turned into something worse, the recurrent bouts of bronchitis and pneumonia visiting their neck of the woods time and time again.

By the time they realized what they were dealing with, they'd been unable to stop it. The fluid in her lungs that last time had been virulent and aggressive, and her tired body could no longer fight the ravages of her disease. Marina had died, obliterating his heart with one swift blow. And his marriage had imploded a year later, when he'd refused to leave his field of medicine.

His wife had protested his decision, saying, "It won't bring Marina back."

It hadn't. But what it had done was destroy any possibility of saving his marriage.

At the time, he'd felt he had no choice. As if his penance was in trying to save other people's children. Even if doing so carved out another little piece of his heart.

Lindy shifted beside him, reminding him that he had a job to do.

So he took a deep breath. "Ready, people? Let's get to work."

And work they did. The patch of infection was the size of a baseball, bigger than he'd originally thought, and it required cutting away more tissue than he'd anticipated. But he wanted to get it all, otherwise it might come back, and none of them wanted that.

Lindy was right beside him, having instruments at hand almost before he asked for them. It was what separated a good surgical nurse from a great one. And she was definitely one of the great ones. Even after having been out of the game for…what had she said? A little over three years?

"Looks like we've gotten it all. We'll ship the tissue off to Pathology and have another culture done."

"It looks good. Really good." Lindy murmured the words over his shoulder.

Her praise sent a burst of warmth through him that had nothing to do with a job well done and everything to do with the stuff that had led to that crazy kiss.

He'd better put a stop to those thoughts right now.

Soon they'd closed the wound, and Zeke breathed a sigh of relief. Part of the patient's aftercare would be IV antibiotics, and the culture would help determine what this particular strain would respond to, although they'd tried most of the broad-spectrum ones already. The ball of infection had lain there unchanged by anything they'd thrown at it. Hopefully manually removing it would make any microbe that remained lose its hold on her.

One of the other nurses took the specimen cup and marked it with their patient's number and date of birth and hand-carried it down to the pathology lab. She called up saying the lab was going to put a rush on the results. "Tell them I said thanks. They can ping my cell when they get it."

"I'll let them know."

Zeke waited until his patient came round, while other members of the team worked on getting their instruments packed away for sterilization.

When they were done, he turned to Lindy. "I could use a coffee. How about you?"

At her slight frown he realized, given the circumstances, he probably shouldn't have asked, but he'd done it out of habit. How many times had he invited whoever happened to be standing around if they wanted to go for coffee? It didn't mean anything, but she evidently thought differently. And maybe it did. But he wasn't going to attempt any big explanations. If she wanted to say no, that was fine.

"Sounds good."

He blinked in surprise but couldn't say he was disappointed by her answer. He liked having company after a difficult surgery. No one had ever taken those invitations to mean anything other than what they were. The camaraderie of teamwork. Sometimes there were seven staff members seated around that table in the hospital cafeteria. And sometimes there were two. He looked around, but the room had basically emptied now that the patient had been wheeled to Recovery, so there was no one else to invite.

He could do this. They were both grown-ups, both capable of getting past one little mistake. Little? Hmm, not according to the dreams that still plagued him at night.

Saying that, he'd rather not have a bunch of people see him having coffee with the new nurse, especially in light of what had happened. So, yes, he'd been stupid to ask. But maybe if they went somewhere else, there would be less cause for tongues to wag.

"I know a coffee shop just down the road from the hospital. It'll get us out in the fresh air for a bit, if you can spare the time."

"I'm due for a half-hour break, so it's fine." But she didn't sound quite as sure as she had a moment ago. Did she think he was asking her out on a date? He didn't want to set her straight and embarrass her, although he had a feeling she had no such illusions.

"Are you up for walking?"

She glanced down at her shoes, which looked comfortable. "I'm good."

Soon they were out the door. "Is it Mulroney's just down the street?"

"Yes. I forgot you're from the area."

He stuffed his hands in his pockets as the full force of the Savannah heat hit him.

"I might need to worry more about melting than what kind of footwear I have on." She laughed as she said it, though.

"I take it you'd rather not have your coffee on the shop's patio?"

"I'd prefer my air to be conditioned, if you don't mind. The cooler the better."

This time he was the one who laughed. "I admit I didn't think this out as well as I might have."

Thankfully, it didn't take long to reach their destination, and the interior of the shop was indeed blessedly cool.

He found a table in a secluded corner of the coffee bar and motioned her to take a seat. A minute later, one of the servers came over and asked for their order. "Go ahead," he said.

"I'd actually like an iced coffee, please, with extra sugar."

His brows went up, but he said nothing, instead ordering his own coffee black and waiting until the server moved away to another customer.

"Would you have ordered that at the hospital cafeteria?"

She smiled. "Have you actually had the coffee there?"

"Have you?"

"No." Her teeth came down on her lip. "I just assumed it was the same as most hospital cafeteria meals. I've come here the last two times I've had a break. I even brought

Daisy here once and ordered her a hot chocolate."

"Your husband never…?"

She didn't ask what he was talking about. "No, never."

There was a tight set to her lips that warned him not to push his luck, so he moved on to a less volatile subject. "Did Mulroney's chocolate get Daisy's stamp of approval?"

"She loved it. My mom actually brought her to meet me that day. She's been great about watching Daisy for me. She insists, actually. I don't blame her. She missed out on a lot."

So had his mom.

His mom had loved Marina, had loved every second of the time they'd spent together. And then after her diagnosis everything had changed.

They'd no longer had entire days to simply let her visit with her grandparents. By that time Marina had been sick more often than not. Their lives had been taken up with fighting an enemy that refused to let go. In the end that enemy had won, and Zeke had lost everything.

His parents had been devastated when they lost not only their granddaughter but also their daughter-in-law. Janice had told them she was sorry, but it hurt too much to stay in contact with them, so she'd dropped out of their lives completely, moving out west.

His mom never said anything directly, but every once in a while she hinted about him remarrying one day. Her ultimate dream was probably another grandchild, especially since she was now alone, his father having died a year ago. She was still grieving his passing.

As for marriage, Zeke didn't see that happening.

After the way he'd shut Janice out during his grief, he'd been wary of relationships. He hadn't liked who he'd become after Marina's death. He'd been selfish and unsupportive, basically crawling into a dark emotional tunnel that only had room for one occupant: him. His wife had been out of luck.

It had been ugly and wrong, and he didn't trust himself to do things differently if faced with a similar crisis. So he didn't try. He wasn't willing to risk someone else's happiness.

And that kiss with Lindy?

It had been a momentary surge of lust. Nothing more. Nothing less. He'd already nipped that in the bud.

"What about you?" Lindy said. "It seems we're always discussing my personal life. What do you do when you're not at the hospital? You're not married…right?"

She was fishing. It made him smile.

"Don't worry, Lindy. You didn't break up a marriage with that kiss. I did that all by myself quite a while ago."

"So you were married?"

"Yep." He already knew what was coming and braced himself for it, although he was surprised she hadn't already heard. There were still some people at the hospital who'd been there at the time of his daughter's illness.

"Any kids?" Her eyes were curious, but there was still no hint that she knew anything about Marina.

What did he tell her? The truth. After all, look at what she'd shared with him.

"I did have. She died five years ago."

"Oh, Zeke, I'm sorry. What happened, if you don't mind my asking?"

"Not at all. She had an incurable lung disease. She died when she was three and a half."

Her hand touched his, but this time it wasn't out of anything other than sympathy. "I didn't know."

"It's not something that comes up in most casual conversations." Was he saying this wasn't that type of conversation? Maybe. Either he was slipping in his old age, or she had a knack for inviting confidences.

Before he could say anything else, their coffees came, and the discussion soon turned to work, and Tessa's case. "Any idea yet when surgery will be?"

"Soon. The hospital is trying to sync their schedules with our open time slots. I imagine it will be sometime this next week after the open house on the women's crisis center."

"She's a sweet little girl."

"Yes. She reminds me of Marina a little bit."

And just like that, he'd circled back around to the subject of his daughter.

"Tell me about her. What was she like?"

"She was a sweet baby. Janice—my wife—and I knew each other in high school and fell in love. Then came med school and all the pressures that came with it. By the time I was done with that and we were ready to have children, nothing seemed to work. We finally went in for fertility treatments and along came Marina. Everything seemed good. At first."

"You said she had a lung condition. Was it asthma?"

"No, an interstitial lung disease. ChILD, to be exact. She had a type called crypto-genic organizing pneumonia, which is just what it sounds like. She had repeated bouts of lung infections until she couldn't fight them off any longer."

"Did you and your wife split over that?"

"About a year after Marina's death. I wasn't a very nice person during that time."

Lindy's head cocked to the side. "What do you mean?"

He could almost see the wheels in her

head turning. "I found out too late that I don't react well to crises. I shut down. Not a trait most women want in a life partner."

"There are worse things."

Looking at it from her point of view, he guessed there were. "Maybe, but in our case it meant the end of our marriage."

"Does it hurt? Treating other people's children, I mean?"

Today's case had been hard. "Sometimes. Especially when the patients are the same age or have a similar illness."

"I can imagine. I'm surprised you still opt to treat those patients."

He shrugged. "How fair would it be of me to refuse to treat a patient simply because it made me sad? Or uncomfortable?"

"I get it." She paused as if thinking. "I get it, but it can't make it any easier."

"No, it doesn't."

They sat in silence for a minute or two, then Lindy sighed and closed her eyes. "They do have great coffee here."

No more confessions? Maybe she was right. There'd been enough soul-baring for one coffee session. And it was probably time to get back.

"I'm not sure about calling a drink with ice 'coffee.'" He smiled to show it wasn't meant as a true criticism.

"Hey, it's made from the same bean that yours is. Like iced tea or hot tea."

He couldn't really argue with that.

The door opened and two nurses from the hospital came in. Lindy recognized them and waved. It served to officially mark the end of personal conversations. And thank God she'd taken her hand off his when their drinks had come. That was all he needed... for the hospital gossip chain to decide to do a little matchmaking based on mistaken assumptions. It was why he hadn't wanted to go to the hospital cafeteria.

Talking about Marina had brought back memories he'd rather have left buried. And to get involved with someone who had a child that was almost the same age as his when she'd died, well, he couldn't imagine it would be good. Or that he wouldn't wonder, year after year, what Marina would have been like at each of those year markers.

Hadn't he already wondered that? His daughter would have been almost nine years old by now. He'd actually looked up a program that could "age" the subject of a photograph. He'd done it with his daughter's picture last year to see what she might have looked like at different stages of her life. He'd printed the images off as a keepsake, but it had been a mistake. The passage of time on those faces had haunted him for months afterward, and he preferred to remember the flesh and blood child, rather than some hazy possibility that would never come to pass. He'd finally had to bury those prints deep inside one of his desk drawers at home. He probably should throw them away, except the thought of doing so felt wrong, like he was throwing away everything that could have been. So he'd kept them. He hadn't thought about those photos for months.

He'd be better off not thinking about them now either.

"My mom is planning to come to the Q&A, even though I told her it was no big deal."

"I don't blame her. She must be proud of how far you've come."

Lindy shrugged. "I'm only mentioning it because she'll want to bring Daisy. Are you planning to show anything graphic?"

"I haven't actually thought about what I'll say, but no. No graphic shots of wounds or anything upsetting."

Although the fact that they even had to have a center like this should be upsetting.

"The hospital has a daycare center for employees. I wasn't sure if you were aware of it. I imagine it will be operating for the Q&A as well, if she wants to drop her off there."

"That's a great idea. It might free up time for my mom, if they take kids on a part-time basis as well. Thanks. And speaking of people in the medical field, I'd probably better get going, I imagine my break is just about up."

"And I need to check on today's surgery patient, so I'd better head back as well." He picked up their trash and tossed it into a nearby waste bin. "And I'll let you know as soon as Tessa's surgery date is set."

"Thanks." She smiled, settling the strap to her purse on her shoulder. "And thanks for suggesting coffee. It was good to get away from the hospital, if only for a few minutes."

"Yes, it was."

And with that, they headed back toward the big white building and the reality that came with it.

CHAPTER FIVE

JUST AS SHE'D SUSPECTED, Lindy's mom had insisted on coming to the Q&A, promising she'd whisk Daisy to the daycare center as soon as the actual meeting started, just in case the conversations became too much for little ears.

Lindy wasn't planning on sharing the worst of the worst, but still it made her nervous to have her mom there.

"Just pretend I'm not here."

"Oh, sure." She smoothed her skirt down over her legs. If she knew her mom, she'd be waving from the audience, which would make it almost impossible to pretend anything.

"And if you want to go out with friends afterward, I can always keep Daisy for the night."

Friends? Was her mom serious?

She barely knew any of these people.

Um…hadn't she kissed one of them?

That didn't count. Besides, she didn't know Zeke any more than she knew anyone else.

Didn't she? She'd told him things that no one else knew, except her parents, and Zeke had shared things about his daughter that he said didn't get thrown around in casual conversations.

Well, after today everyone in the room would know the basics of what had happened to her, but she certainly wasn't going to get it tattooed across her forehead.

She glanced at the clock and saw there were only ten minutes until she was on.

"Okay, Mom, I should probably go."

"Love you. I'll take our girl out in a few minutes." Rachel kissed her on the cheek and settled into a chair with Daisy on her lap.

By the time Lindy got to the front, Zeke was already beside the podium, talking to a group of people. So was Neil, the hospital administrator. He waved her over.

Taking a deep breath, she smiled and joined them. Were they already volunteers, or were they new to the program like she was?

Dressed in tan khakis and a snug black polo that hugged his biceps, Zeke looked confident and unruffled. A world away from the nervous slosh of stomach acid she was currently dealing with.

"You look nice," he murmured.

A rush of warmth flooded her face. Great. Just what she needed.

"So do you."

And her mom, right on cue, was holding Daisy up and using her hand to move her granddaughter's in the semblance of a wave.

Ugh. So much for presenting a professional appearance.

She pulled herself up short. This wasn't about professionalism. This was about helping women. Women like she'd once been.

Neil nodded at the podium. "Once people take their seats, I'll open with some introductions and then you're on, okay?"

"That's fine." She was as ready as she'd ever be.

"Princess!" Daisy's voice rang out across the gathering, causing a quick burst of laughter.

Oh, brother. Why had she ever thought having her mom here was a good idea? Oh, wait. She hadn't thought that. Not once.

If that wasn't bad enough, her mom was suddenly up front, mingling with the other hospital employees. "Look, Daisy, there's the man you ate lunch with." Rachel turned to Lindy and whispered, "Isn't his name Zeke, or something like that?"

"Yes, but—"

Zeke had moved a short distance away to talk to someone else.

"Let's go say hi. You can tell him about your new princess castle."

"Princess!"

Lindy broke into her daughter's mounting excitement before it got out of hand. "I don't think that's a good idea. I'm sure he's busy."

"Nonsense. I'm sure he'll be happy to see Daisy again." And before Lindy could say anything else, the pair sauntered off, leaving her to groan out loud.

"Mothers."

"Ain't it the truth?" A voice to her side made her look. Nancy, a glass of some type of cola in her hand, smiled at the consternation on her face. "They drive you crazy, but you wouldn't trade them for the world."

"I don't know. Today might be the day…"

They both laughed, and Lindy glanced at her. Maybe the thing about not having made any friends wasn't entirely true. She and Nancy had shared a few moments of chitchat here and there. "Are you interested in volunteering if the center opens?"

"Yep. I have a vested interest, since my baby sister is in a bad relationship and won't leave."

"I'm so sorry." Lindy bit her lip. Not to stop herself from sharing her story but out of embarrassment. She'd once been like that baby sister. And Nancy was going to hear her talk about it soon enough.

"I'm hoping one day she'll realize."

"I do too."

She glanced up to see Zeke staring at her and realized he was holding Daisy. Oh, no. She'd never seen a man look any more uncomfortable than he did right now.

Then it hit her. He no longer had a daughter to hold. And to have Daisy thrust at him like a sack of potatoes…

Her mom had no idea, though, because her mouth was moving a mile a minute just as Daisy threw her arms around Zeke's neck and squeezed.

That was her cue.

"Will you excuse me? I think I have to rescue Dr. Bruen before he passes out."

Nancy giggled. "He does look a little odd. His face is beet red."

"Yes, it is." She made her way through the small groups of people who were conversing, hoping she could get up there before Zeke made some kind of "no-kids" rule for any future meetings, not that he made those kinds of decisions.

She arrived and held her arms out. "Sorry, Zeke. I'll take her."

"It's okay. Your mom was just telling me about your new place. It sounds charming."

She turned toward her mom and gave her a hard look. "It is. But I'm sure you must have other things to do than chat about my living conditions."

"On the contrary. I'm way down on the program so I have plenty of time to kill. Besides, Rachel and Daisy are keeping me from becoming too nervous."

That was the funniest thing she'd heard all day. He was a well-respected surgeon who commanded the operating room the way a ship's captain commanded his vessel. There was no way he would be scared to face a group and talk about what he did on a daily basis.

"I have my doubts about that."

He smiled. "Now, Daisy, on the other hand, wants me to dress up as a princess with her. That does make me nervous."

Oh, Lord. She should have known. How many times had she had to dress in one of her best party dresses in order to have tea with her pint-sized daughter?

"I'm sure. Although that could be an interesting look." She smiled at Zeke, letting her nerves settle. Maybe the look he'd thrown her hadn't been one of horror after all. She'd offered to take Daisy and he hadn't taken her up on it. Although he was right. Lindy was the first one to present.

Lindy's mom chimed in. "We'll have to have you over for dinner sometime. I'm sure both Daisy and Lindy would love that."

It seemed that with every word she uttered her mom was digging her daughter into a hole and had no idea she was throwing another shovelful of dirt on the growing pile.

"I'm sure Daisy would. I'm not so sure about Lindy," was all Zeke said, throwing a quick smile in her direction.

"Well, I guess this princess had better find her way to the daycare center." Her mom held out her arms. "I'll have Lindy get with you about a date for dinner."

"Do that."

Oh, Lord, why did her mom have to have that ingrained Southern hospitality? And she was so gently insistent that it was the rare person who got offended by it. It was just the way she was. Lindy had learned to appreciate it, for the most part, even if she hadn't quite embraced the trait.

By the time her mom moved away, Neil was asking everyone to find a seat. He presented the basics about what the hospital hoped to do, going over the funding that had already been secured, then went over the list of presenters, which included herself, two of the hospital's resident psychiatrists and Zeke. Once they'd finished, the floor would be open to questions.

Her mom slid back in the room and took a seat in the back just as Neil was finishing up.

"A sign-up sheet will be in the back for anyone interested in giving a few hours of their time. The ultimate fate of the program rests in your hands. And on that note, I'll turn the floor over to Lindy Franklin, who is new to Mid Savannah but certainly not new to working in this type of program." He nodded at her. "Lindy?"

The nerves that had been settled suddenly rose to her throat and threatened to choke her. Then she caught sight of Zeke. Maybe he saw the hint of panic in her face because he edged forward until he was standing just behind her elbow. But far enough away that those around them would simply think he was waiting for his turn.

Just knowing he was there helped her get

through the rough patch and she cleared her throat. "Hello, everyone."

A spatter of returned greetings made her smile, and then she was fine. "As Neil said, my name is Lindy Franklin and I am indeed new here. But what he didn't tell you is that I was once the victim of domestic violence."

She watched people shift in their seats as they took in her words. Nancy looked shocked, as did some of the other nurses she worked with. "Most of you didn't know that about me, and that's at the heart of the problem. Most victims will never speak out about what is happening. They rarely seek help. But if they know help is there, it becomes a safety net. One that people like I was desperately need."

She talked about some of the things she wished she'd known when she'd been with Luke and ways to get the word out to others.

Lindy ended by saying, "We want Savannah to know that help is available. It's free. It's confidential. And we can help you get out. Thank you."

Applause went up and Nancy gave her a

thumbs-up sign, while her mom was dabbing at her eyes with a tissue.

Both of the hospital's psychiatrists came up and took her place, discussing between them the psychology of abuse, referencing several things she'd said and using them as illustrations.

"Good job, Lind." Zeke's low voice filtered through, carrying with it a note of admiration. "If what I saw out there is any indication, this program is really going to take off. I'd be surprised if we didn't get fifty volunteers right off the bat."

She'd spoken from her heart, but surely it hadn't made that much of a difference.

You just need to give that wheel a push to get it moving.

Then it was Zeke's turn. And wow. Just wow. He told the story of Meredith Brewster's injuries, being careful to keep any identifying elements out of his speech. But listening to him, she remembered the horror she'd felt on learning a five-year-old child had had to deal with a horrific injury at the hands of a parent. She looked around the room. No one was shifting or looking around. Even her mom was totally caught up in what he was saying. True to his word, he didn't give any of the gory details, but he still got his point across. At the end of his speech, the applause was almost deafening.

Neil moved forward, shaking Zeke's hand and murmuring something to him before turning to the audience. "Thank you to our staff for taking time out of their busy schedules to talk to us. And thank you for being here. We'd like to hear any questions or comments you might have. If you like what you've heard, there are packets stacked at the door that have a list of helpful numbers. And as I mentioned earlier, there's also a sign-up sheet, if you'd like to help this program get off the ground." He glanced at Lindy. "Let me say one more thing. If you feel someone's life is in immediate danger, I would urge you not to wait but to call 911."

The presenters fielded questions between them, with Lindy getting more than her share. She answered as best she could, grateful that everyone was respectful about not asking specifics about her own situation.

Twenty minutes later there were no more lifted hands.

"Any other questions?" Neil asked, scanning the group for hands. She kept hers firmly down, even as his eyes slid over her and kept going. "Well, I guess that's it. There are refreshments at the back. Help yourselves and thanks again for letting us take up your time. If you're due back on the floor, please make your way there."

And then it was over. Zeke bumped her shoulder and gave her a smile. "Thanks for asking me to come. I think the hospital is going to do some great things with the program."

"I do too." The casual nudge had made her feel warm and tingly inside. It felt like they were finding their way back to where they'd started. Before that kiss had derailed things.

She spotted her mom, who'd evidently already picked Daisy up from daycare, coming through the door. She glanced back, to see that Zeke was just behind her. "I wanted to say bye to your mom and Daisy."

She smiled. "I'm sure they'll like that."

Rachel spoke up when they got there. "I was just about to suggest Lindy and Daisy come to the house for popcorn and a movie later tonight. You're invited as well."

Well, since she hadn't even given Lindy a chance to say yes or no to her own invitation, it was a bit forward of her to start inviting other people.

"I can't tonight, I'm sorry. I have other plans, but I'd like a raincheck on that dinner invitation you talked about earlier."

"Of course. That's a given. Well, I guess we'll have to watch *The Princess Bride* without you."

"Princess, huh? Looks like I'm missing out. By the way, a little girl gave me a packet of princess stickers that I think Daisy will probably get more use out of than I will."

"Princess!"

"I'll be kind of glad when we move into the martial arts stage," Lindy muttered.

He tilted his head. "Martial arts?"

Lindy laughed. "Basically anything other than princesses. But I'm sure she would love the stickers, thanks for thinking of her."

"I don't have anyone else to entrust them

to." A brief shadow went through his dark eyes before it was gone. Remembering his own daughter?

A shard of pain went through her chest. She didn't know what she would do if she ever lost Daisy…didn't even want to think of that possibility. But she wasn't immune from tragedy, she'd already proven that. But surely she had been through the worst that life had to throw at her. Hadn't she?

She knew no one could guarantee that they'd be exempt from tragedy, but she was pretty sure most parents would trade places in a second if they could take away the pain from their child. She imagined Zeke had made all kinds of promises to God, asking Him to spare his daughter. He'd probably even offered his own life up instead.

Except Lindy couldn't imagine a world where Zeke didn't exist, even though she'd only known him a matter of weeks.

Did he still have contact with his ex-wife? Had they divided Marina's things or pictures to remember her by? How heartbreaking would that be during a divorce? Had they squabbled about what things the other could have and what they wanted to keep for themselves?

Lindy hadn't had to go through that. Even if Luke had lived, he'd have been in prison. And the courts would have made sure he had no contact with his daughter ever again.

"Anyway, she'll love them, thank you. I'll get a sticker book for her to put them in."

"I forgot they had books. I'd like to pick one up if I could."

A dangerous prickling started behind her eyes. She blinked it away, but when she found her voice she was horrified to hear a slight waver in it. "You don't have to do that." She didn't want to be the cause of stirring up painful memories. Her parents had tiptoed around the subject of Luke since she'd been home. They knew kind of what had happened, but she'd never told them about the choking incident.

The only people who knew were the police, actually. And the medical professionals that had checked her trachea for damage and swelling. And the bruising… She'd waited for it to subside before she'd packed her things and headed home. For her parents to see that would have been too much. Her dad would have blamed himself for not coming after her. But she might not have left any earlier than she had, and it could have put him in danger as well.

"I'd like to, unless you'd rather I didn't."

"Of course not." She tried to tell him with her eyes that it wasn't necessary, but he simply smiled her concern away. And then her mom kissed Daisy on the cheek and with a quick glance at both of them said she wanted to stop at the store and get some popcorn for their movie night.

"Mom, I can do that."

"No, I'm sure you need to finalize things here." She looked at Zeke. "If you change your mind about coming, have Lindy give you the address. If you've never seen *The Princess Bride* you're missing out. It's quite funny, even for adults."

"I'll keep that in mind. And thank you again for the invitation."

No mention this time of having plans. Had that all been a crock?

"I'll see you in about an hour, Lindy."

Knowing it would do no good to argue with her mother, she nodded.

Once they were out of earshot, Lindy looked at him with what she hoped was a rueful expression. "I am so sorry about that. She doesn't get that not everyone is all about watching movies with her granddaughter."

"She's proud of her, as she should be."

He was right, of course. "Well, I am sorry she pressured you into coming over to the house. She won't be offended if you don't come, especially since you have plans." It was meant as a gentle reminder of what he'd said earlier.

"I did have something planned, but I think I've changed my mind about doing it."

He gave no more explanation than that, so she didn't know if the plans had involved someone else. A date, maybe?

That thought made her heart cramp as a million images marched past her mind's eye, each worse than the one before it. Zeke kissing other women, trailing his fingers over their bodies. Moving over them as he…

Stop it! Of course the man dated. He'd be crazy not to.

Hmm…*she* didn't date. Did that make her crazy?

That was different.

Before she could respond, Zeke went on, "If the offer is still open, I think I might like to see this famed movie."

"Y-you do?" She'd gotten the impression he wasn't eager to spend time with her outside work, so what had changed? And did she even want it to change? But she couldn't very well retract the offer without having some kind of explanation available, and right now those were in short supply. "Um, okay, Daisy will be ecstatic. If she can even stay awake. She tends to nod off halfway through."

He gave her a quick look. "Are you okay with it? I don't want to intrude. These meetings are always hard to get through. The reality of what people go through…" He stopped as if realizing who he was talking to. "I'm glad you got away."

"Thank you. I am too. I'm swearing off relationships, though, for a long time."

"I've sworn them off too, so we're even.

So, are we good? A movie as colleagues and friends?"

Friends? Wow. A warm mushy feeling crept up from somewhere deep inside her. She'd just been thinking about the fact that she didn't have many friends here yet...that she hadn't had time to develop any, and now Zeke and Nancy had both stepped a little closer. And as much as she didn't want to, she found that she liked it. A little too much.

CHAPTER SIX

ZEKE KNEW EXACTLY why he'd accepted Rachel's invitation. His plans for that evening had revolved around a resolution he'd made as he held Daisy before the open house. He'd originally been pretty horrified when Lindy's mom had thrust the little girl into his arms, but nothing had prepared him for the feeling that erupted when Daisy threw her arms around his neck.

Since Lindy said she'd walked to work that day, they drove to buy popcorn together. The plan was for Zeke to drop her and Daisy off at her house when they were done with the movie. It was on his way home anyway. And Lindy had said if an emergency came up and he needed to leave, she'd just stay with her folks and have them take her home the next day.

"Daisy's in the kitchen with her Mimi" said the man who'd opened the door.

Lindy made quick introductions and her dad, Harold, shook his hand.

"Nice to meet you."

Letting Lindy lead the way, he entered a home.

Not just a house, like his and Janice's had been on too many occasions, even after Marina was born, but a genuine home, filled with warmth and pictures and memorabilia of Lindy's time as a child.

It was much like the home he'd grown up in.

Why had he and Janice done so little of that? He wasn't sure, but it made him wonder if there hadn't been a crack in the foundation of their relationship even before Marina had come along. Her death had just split it wide open and exposed it for what it was.

Looking back, he wondered if he should have taken his ex-wife's advice and kept some of his daughter's belongings. Instead, he had little more than a few ragged photos and several age progression images. Which was what his so-called plans had originally involved this evening. He'd been going to search for them until he found them, and then he was going to shred them.

And that made him a coward. Because the only reason he'd come here was to avoid doing something he probably should have done long ago. Because thinking of all the might-have-beens had eaten at him for the last five years.

And yet here he was, spending time with a family that highlighted everything he'd lost. Wasn't that adding torture to torture?

He didn't know, but it was too late to back out now. He could feign an emergency at the hospital, but he'd already committed to staying for the movie and he wasn't willing to throw the invitation back in Rachel's face after she'd seemed so happy that he'd changed his mind.

He felt a little ludicrous sitting on a couch with a family he didn't really know, watching a film and eating popcorn. But it was ludicrous in a good kind of way. He ate a bite, and then another, and watched the crazy antics of the characters on the screen. In the end it was a movie about falling in love, just like a million other movies he'd watched over his lifetime. But this time it was different somehow.

Daisy stretched out and pushed her socked feet against the arm of the sofa, forcing Lindy over until her leg was pressed against his. "Sorry," she whispered, trying to pull away.

Except she couldn't. And he was against his side of the couch with nowhere else to go. The temptation to slide his arm around her came and went without incident. But not without a trickle of awareness that went almost unnoticed at first. Almost. But not entirely.

She might be sorry, but he wasn't. At least not yet. Right now he was enjoying that low steady hum. The one that lingered just below the surface of his mind, waiting for permission to grow and become bolder. Zeke had no intention of granting that permission, but it was nice to imagine what might happen if he did.

The banter between two of the characters made Daisy chortle loudly. Lindy gave a choked giggle in return. "Sorry," she whispered again. "She loves this movie, especially the sword fight."

"Sword fight, huh?"

He couldn't hold back a smile. And suddenly the hum grew in intensity, egged on by her whispered words and how they were meant for his ears and his alone. Despite being in the middle of her parents' living room, it was as if they were cocooned in their own little bubble of a world. He could see her folks sitting in their chairs, facing away from them as they watched the movie, but they were like so much background noise. As was Daisy, despite her laugh.

Was he the only one who felt it? Or did Lindy sense it as well?

He hoped so, because he was going to feel incredibly stupid if he was the only one who was getting an emotional buzz out of her proximity.

Then a slight sonorous noise came from beside him. He glanced at Lindy, wondering how she could have fallen asleep. But it wasn't her. It was Daisy. She was lying half across her mother's lap, mouth open, making tiny gargling sounds. He chuckled. A second ago, the child had been wide awake.

"Told you," Lindy whispered again, and his innards ratcheted another notch tighter.

"Yes, you did." He kept his own voice just as quiet, not wanting her parents to turn around and see them with their heads close, talking in quiet whispers. Heaven only knew what kind of ideas they would get from that.

Heaven only knew what kind of ideas *he* was going to get.

And that continued pressure of her thigh against his wasn't helping matters. If he wasn't careful, he was going to give them some concrete evidence that he'd rather they not see. The physical attraction was there without a doubt, but Zeke had no intention of letting it go any further than that. Because juxtaposed against the sweet, sweet press of her leg was the reality of Daisy and how it made him ache for Marina. And would likely continue to make him ache with the passing of years.

Someday he was going to have to face throwing away those age progression pictures he'd made. But today was evidently not the day.

"How long is this movie?" he asked.

"We're about halfway through. Everything okay?" She again tried to shift her leg away, but Daisy's feet were still firmly planted against the arm. It looked like she wouldn't budge.

"Fine. And don't worry about moving her."

"I thought you might be getting claustrophobic."

He was getting something, but it definitely wasn't claustrophobia."

"No." On the other side of the attraction issue was the sense that it felt right having her against him, and Zeke didn't want that at all. Because it wasn't "right." None of it was. It was an illusion that would go up in a puff of smoke as soon as they were back in their respective homes.

At least that's what he told himself. It was the only thing currently keeping him sane.

Time to concentrate on the movie. Then he realized that Harold's head had canted sideways, and a sound louder than Daisy's assailed his ears. He glanced at Lindy and she nodded. "Yep. He always falls asleep. I think that's where Daisy gets it from."

And that did it. Zeke put his arm around her, and Lindy melted against him as if she'd been waiting for that all evening.

Had she?

All too soon, the couple got their weird, but happy, ending and he unhooked his arm, pulling it back to his side before they got caught and had to give some kind of explanation. As it was, no one noticed.

Rachel was too busy shaking Harold awake. He grumbled and acted like he'd been watching the film all along. Lindy giggled. "Something else that happens all the time."

Okay. And that was his sign to get up.

In a minute. His right leg had fallen asleep from the way they'd been sitting, but he hadn't wanted to make her move. He still didn't.

Lindy's mom stretched. "Why don't you all stay the night?"

His gut seized. What was she saying? She

wanted him to spend the night with Lindy and the rest of the brood?

As in the same room?

"Mom, Zeke has his own house." Lindy smiled to take the sting out of it. "And so do I."

"Yes, I'll take Daisy and Lindy home and then head back to my place."

"Are you sure?" Rachel insisted.

Lindy saved him from answering. "Yes, we are, aren't we, Zeke?"

Well, she didn't save him entirely.

"Lindy's right on my way so yes. Thank you for the hospitality, though. And the popcorn." He held up his mostly empty bowl. "Where do you want me to put this?"

"I'll take it." Rachel held her hand out. "And thank you for coming. We're really glad you changed your mind."

Zeke stood, pushing his khakis down over his legs.

Harold nodded and shook his hand, grip firm, even after falling asleep. "Come back any time."

"Thank you, sir. I will."

Lindy was still sitting on the sofa, pinned

beneath Daisy's slight frame. Rachel moved forward as if to help, but Zeke got there first. "Here, let me take her."

He hefted the child into his arms, surprised that someone so small could feel so solid. It was good. Felt right.

There were those words again. Words he needed to banish from his vocabulary.

Lindy stood, stretching her back. "I think my whole right side is asleep."

The same thing he'd thought about his leg. It made him smile. "This little thing cut off your circulation?"

"You try holding her for a two-hour movie and see how you feel afterward. Although I wouldn't trade it for the world."

He remembered those days. In fact, the memories of those days had helped him get through the worst of his grief.

"Are you sure about driving us home? I'm sure one of my parents could."

"Like I said, it's on my way. And it'll save your mom a trip there and back."

Lindy switched the car seat from Rachel's car and installed it in his while he held Daisy. "I'll give it back to her tomorrow when she picks us up."

He lowered Daisy into her car seat and carefully buckled her in. Despite the passing of years, he still remembered how to secure a child in their seat.

They were soon on their way, getting onto the highway.

"Thanks again, Zeke. I hope we weren't too boring for you. I'm sure your Friday nights are normally much more exciting."

"Not really. My plans weren't with friends, just myself. I had some things I wanted to catch up on. But that can happen another time. The movie was cute."

"It's a classic. Kind of slapstick humor, but it grows on you."

Kind of like having her beside him had grown on him. A little too much actually.

She leaned back and stretched, the act making her breasts jut out. "I have about a thousand kinks in my spine."

He swallowed, hoping he wasn't about to get a kink in something else. Having her plastered against him had been the best kind of torture. His nerve endings hadn't completely recovered. Maybe they wouldn't until she was out of the car.

"You've been on your feet most of the day, then had the question and answer session and then movie night. It's no wonder."

"Hmm...and your day has been so much lighter?" The words came with a smile and raised brows.

"Okay, we've both had a full day."

"At least I'm off tomorrow. You?"

"I am as well. I try not to work Sundays if I don't have to."

She turned to look at him. "You go to church?"

"Sometimes. My taking off Sundays isn't for religious reasons, though. It's more personal."

When she tilted her head, he knew he was going to tell her, although he wasn't exactly sure why. Maybe it was the time spent at her parents'. Maybe it was the arm he'd draped around her shoulders. But right now he felt connected to her in a way that made him trust her.

"Marina died on a Sunday. It's been long enough ago that I could probably work now, but it's just become a habit. So I've continued it."

A sense of relief whooshed over him when she didn't react in a way that made him feel ridiculous. Instead she covered his hand with hers as it lay on the gear shift. "I think that's a great idea. We all need rest. And it kind of makes her day sacred and ensures she's remembered. I think Marina would like it."

"Thanks." A lump formed in his throat that had nothing to do with his daughter's death. Lindy had endured her own tragedy and yet she was able to see past it to other people's suffering. Maybe he should try being a little more like her.

She glanced behind her to the back seat. "I can't believe she's still asleep. I hope this doesn't mean she'll be up at the crack of dawn. I wouldn't mind sleeping in for once."

An image of Lindy waking up slid into his mind. Brown eyes blinking open, a slow smile on her face as she peered up sleepily...

At him.

And there it was. The stupidity that he couldn't seem to shake. With each instance it seemed to embed itself deeper into his brain, making it harder and harder to shake.

Hell, he was a surgeon. Shouldn't he be able to cut it out, the same way he was going to dissect the mass in Tessa's stomach?

That was evidently beyond his purview. He could operate on real people, but not on himself.

He suddenly realized Lindy was looking at him—waiting for an answer to her statement.

"Daisy's had a pretty big day. We all have."

They arrived at her house a few minutes later. When he started to get out of the car, she said, "I can get her."

"I'm sure you can, but it'll be easier if I help. Plus we have the car seat."

"Oh, that's right."

Exiting the vehicle, he opened the passenger door and undid the straps of Daisy's car seat. "Do you want me to get her or the seat?"

She hesitated. "You decide."

"How about if you unlock the door and I'll carry her in and then come back out and get the car seat?"

"Are you sure?"

He was already lifting the sleeping child out of the seat. Lindy watched for a second, then suddenly spun around and headed up the walk, digging in her purse for something. Probably her keys.

By the time he got to the door, it was standing open, with Lindy beckoning him inside. "It's this way."

He followed her into the house and down a hallway. She turned on lights as they went. Then she opened a door and pressed a switch, but the lights must have been on a dimmer switch because the room didn't erupt in a blast of light. Instead it was soft and muted. He saw a toddler bed over to the right and headed there as Lindy pulled down the covers.

He padded over to the bed and carefully laid Daisy down. If this had been Marina, he would have kissed her goodnight. But it wasn't, and it wasn't for him to tuck her in. He took a step back and let Lindy do the honors. And just as he would have expected, she leaned down and kissed her daughter on the forehead before tucking the light covers around her. She put a finger to her lips.

Ha! He wasn't about to say anything, so no worries there.

She tiptoed out of the room and shut the door behind her.

"Is she a light sleeper?"

She smiled. "No. That girl could sleep through a hurricane, I believe."

"That makes it nice for you."

"Yes. She's always been a good sleeper, even as a baby."

Then she shut her eyes. "Sorry. You don't need to hear about that."

"About what?"

"Nothing. Can I get you some coffee? A glass of wine?"

"No wine. A beer would be nice, if you have one."

"I do, actually, although it's light. Is that okay?"

"That's actually perfect, since I'm driving home." Light beer had a lower alcohol content than the regular version. Those calories had to be cut from somewhere, didn't they?

"Why don't you sit in the living room

while I get them? I could use a glass of wine to unwind."

Instead of going into the other room like she'd suggested, he followed her into the kitchen while she popped open the refrigerator and emerged with a long-necked bottle and some wine.

"Do you want yours in a glass?"

"Nope. I'll drink it straight up."

He waited for her to get a wine glass down from a tall glass-fronted cupboard and then took the bottle opener she handed him. He popped the top on his beer and the contents of the bottle made a satisfying hiss as the carbonation was released. He took a long pull and followed her into the other room.

"I haven't finished furnishing the place."

She was right. The living room consisted of a sofa, a coffee table and a television set.

Which meant he was going to have to sit next to her. Again. But at least he wouldn't have a child shoving them against each other.

He'd already been desensitized to her proximity during the movie. Right?

Somehow he didn't think so. But rather

than looking like a coward for standing while she sat, he eased himself down onto the sofa, grabbing a coaster and setting his drink on it.

"Nice place."

"My parents helped me find it." Her lips twisted, and she took a sip of her wine, kicking her shoes off and tucking her feet under her. She turned toward him. "Actually, they helped me in a lot of ways. They offered to let me keep living with them until I could get back on my feet, but their house is small, and I thought I'd be in the way with Daisy. They love her dearly, but I felt they needed to be able to have some semblance of privacy, although she still takes up a lot of their lives. It's worked out, though."

He picked up his beer and took another slug, the brew tasting good as it went down. "So you like your job at the hospital?"

"I love it more than you can know."

"Oh, I think I already know. If it's anything like the way I feel about surgery, then it's irreplaceable. It has its drawbacks and heartbreaks, but for the most part I couldn't ask for a better life."

There was a photo of her and Daisy on top of the television. Lindy was in a hospital gown and she was holding Daisy in her arms. There was no sign of her ex. Maybe he was the one who'd taken the shot, although he couldn't imagine Lindy wanting to keep the picture if that was the case.

He could remember his ex holding Marina when life had been simple and still filled with happiness. But in the end they just hadn't been able to cope with the loss as a couple.

A thought came to mind. "I got a text during the open house about Tessa's surgery. It's scheduled for Tuesday. Do you still want to be on the roster?"

"Yes. Please." She wrapped her hand around her bare feet and tugged them in closer.

Her toes were tipped in some kind of silvery glitter polish that he hadn't noticed when she'd first taken her shoes off. It was not a color choice he would have expected her to wear, and he found himself fascinated by the way the flecks of color caught the light. "Interesting choice in nail polish."

She glanced down and smiled. "Sometimes I like to be a little wild and crazy. Just because I can."

He'd almost forgotten. There'd evidently been a time when she couldn't express herself without fear of recriminations. But over something as simple as nail polish? "Did he control that too?"

"No, not really. But there were times he'd ridicule my decisions if they didn't fit in with who he thought I should be."

"And who did he think you should be?"

"I was never quite sure. Maybe the perfect little wife. But I was the wrong person to choose, then, because I'm so far from perfect that it's not even funny."

"Oh, I don't know. I don't think you're that far off the mark."

He hadn't meant to say that. As her eyes came up and met his, he saw a flurry of emotions go by in quick succession. Then she smiled. "You obviously don't know me very well if you can say that. And I remember when you were worried that I couldn't keep up with the surgical department."

"Like you said, I obviously didn't know

you back then. Because you keep up just fine."

"You didn't know me back then, but you do now?"

A strange expectancy hung in the air between them, and he wasn't sure what she wanted him to say. Or if she wanted him to say anything at all.

He was torn. He did feel like he'd gotten to know her over the last weeks. And that was part of the problem. Part of what made him keep circling back toward her, even when he wanted nothing more than to fly far away.

"I think maybe I'm coming to."

"I think maybe I'm coming to know you too. You're not quite the ogre I thought you were in the beginning."

His brows went up. "You thought I was an ogre?"

"Well…maybe ogre is too strong a word. But I was a little intimidated by you."

In the same way her husband had intimidated her? He didn't like that. He propped his arm on the back of the couch. "I don't normally have that effect on people. At least I hope I don't."

Even when he'd been at his worst, Janice hadn't been afraid of him.

"It was me. You've been great, and I appreciate it." She leaned a little closer and the heat from her body slid in and made his muscles loosen and then slowly tighten again.

He thought for a minute she might lay her head on his shoulder. He swallowed, suddenly wanting her to do exactly that. He wanted her pressed tight against him like she'd been at her parents' house. Only this time there'd be no one to see them.

Maybe that was his cue to leave.

Except she chose that very moment to tip her head back and look into his eyes. What he saw there made him stay exactly where he was, his breath stalling in his lungs long enough to make him feel woozy. Then it pumped in a full load of oxygen, sending it throughout his body in a rush of endorphins that made him want to do the unthinkable.

Time to break the spell. "Tell me it's time to go."

The fingers behind her on the sofa went to her shoulder and cupped it.

"Do you want to go?"

That was a loaded question if ever he'd heard one. He tipped his beer from side to side. "My bottle's empty."

She licked her lips. "So is my glass. Do you want another one?"

"No. I don't."

"Then what *do* you want?"

That was a tricky question, because what he wanted didn't come in a bottle. Or a glass. He should repeat that he wanted to leave, but somehow he couldn't force the words out.

He touched a finger to the polish on one of her toes. "I want to be like this nail polish."

"I don't understand."

"I want to be wild and crazy. Just because I can. Isn't that what you said?"

"Yes," she whispered. "It is."

"So if I did something wild and crazy… what would you do?"

"It depends what it is."

His brain told him to stop right here, even

as something else told him to keep on going. "'It' would be kissing you."

She gave him a slow smile. "Then I might have to do something a little wild and crazy too. Like kiss you back."

"Honey, that is what I was hoping you'd say."

And with that, he did something he'd been wanting to do ever since that day in his office. And again on her parents' sofa. He drew her close and planted his mouth on hers.

CHAPTER SEVEN

SHE'D THOUGHT THEIR first kiss had been out of this world?

Well, nothing could have prepared her for the sudden overload of sensations—the heady extravagance—of finding his lips on hers again. Why had she ever thought avoiding this was the smart thing to do?

Even as he drew her closer, her arms snaked around his neck and she gave herself fully to the kiss. It was what she wanted. What she needed. And just like her nail polish it was wild and crazy and just for her. She deserved a night of wanton sex. Sex that was offered with open arms and freely accepted.

She moaned when his tongue slid inside her mouth, the sweet friction sending goosebumps dancing across her body. A body that could rapidly grow used to his touch. His tongue eased back, and she was suddenly afraid he was going to take that away from her. Her hand went to the back of his head as if to hold him there. He surged forward again, and the burst of pleasure it brought was almost too much to bear.

Zeke was all she wanted right now.

Her fingers twined in the hair at his nape, and what she'd thought of as slightly long before became the perfect length. She tightened her fingers and felt him smile against her mouth.

When he pulled back, her eyes opened in a rush, afraid he was going to leave after all.

Instead, his thumb rubbed across her lower lip, the lip that was now hyper-sensitized to his touch. "Are you wild and crazy enough to let me stay? Just for tonight?"

"Yes."

He scooped her up in his arms and stood, his mouth descending for another swift kiss before saying, "Where?"

"I don't care. You choose."

"I would say right here, but I want complete privacy. I don't want some small visitor wandering in."

He was right. She didn't want that either. "My bedroom is the last door on the left."

That was all he needed evidently. He strode down the hallway, his steps light but sure, quick but not rushed. Was that what his lovemaking would be like?

She gulped. She wasn't sure she could wait.

And then they were inside. He pushed the door shut with his foot and turned them to face it. "Lock it, Lind."

She did, although her fingers trembled slightly as she turned the latch.

He walked to the bed and dropped her on it without warning. She bounced a time or two, making her laugh. The laughter died when he leaned over her, hands landing on either side of her on the bed.

God.

A quick flash of muscle memory made her freeze, before her heart and mind set her straight.

She wasn't trapped. If she asked him to stand up, he would. She blinked, and Zeke's face was all she saw. He was sexy, strong and so very intense. But he was also kind and gentle. He'd asked permission every step of the way, had taken nothing for granted.

He was what she needed. What she wanted.

Her bare feet went to the backs of his knees, the fabric from his khaki slacks smooth and cool against her soles. Then his arms folded until he was down on his elbows, and he kissed her again, making all those heady sensations from the living room come roaring back to life. But only for a second, then he was up and off her again.

When she started to protest he held up a finger and then reached down to haul his shirt over his head.

The man was taut and tanned and altogether too gorgeous for his own good, and she had no idea why he'd decided she was the one he wanted to spend the night with, but she was damned glad he had.

She sat up, not wanting this to be one-sided. She wanted tonight to be about give-and-take. She unbuttoned the first two buttons of her blouse then fumbled with the third for half a second, before he came to the rescue, slowly undoing one after the other, then tugging the bottom of it out of her skirt. He peeled it off her torso, and then he swallowed with a jerky movement of his Adam's apple. "You're beautiful, Lind. So very beautiful."

The sudden prick of tears behind her eyes was altogether unexpected.

He leaned down with a frown, one of his thumbs brushing at an area of moisture and carrying it away. "What's wrong?"

"Nothing. Nothing's wrong. I promise." She reached up and cupped his face, breathing in his scent and letting it sift down to the part of her brain where her long-term memories were stored. She dropped it there, never wanting to forget tonight. Then she shrugged out of her shirt and threw it toward the footboard. "Take me to bed, Zeke."

It was kind of a ridiculous statement since they were already in bed, but she trusted him to know what she meant.

He did, because his fingers went to his belt and pulled the tab through the buckle, the metal clink of the tongue making her shiver with anticipation. He pulled his wallet out of his pocket and drew out protection, tossing it onto the bed beside her.

She hadn't had to ask. He'd just taken care of the obvious.

God. She needed to tread with care, because it wouldn't take much for her to fall for this man. And that's the last thing she needed in her life right now, just when she was starting to find herself. But for tonight she could soak in his presence and luxuriate in what he was going to do for her. Without guilt. Without recriminations.

Then he was shedding his trousers, kicking them away from him and standing there in snug black briefs that did nothing to hide what she was making him feel. What he was making *her* feel.

Her hands went to his lean hips, letting herself explore the skin above his waistband, a ripple of muscles under her touch making her smile. "Tickle?"

"Mmm, yes, but in the best kind of way." His voice was low with a hint of gravel that made her mouth water. She did that to him.

And she wanted it all. Wanted to explore and taste and take everything he had to offer.

She tunneled her fingers beneath the elastic waistband and around to his butt, giving it a squeeze. A low groan from him told her he liked what she was doing.

Pushing the undergarment down, easing it over the tense flesh and letting it spring free, she couldn't help but stare. She was drunk. But it wasn't from the wine she'd had. Zeke intoxicated her, made her feel wild and free.

Her hands went back to his hips and then she leaned forward, her mouth sliding over him in a rush, his quick epithet following soon after. But it did nothing to stop her. Instead, it drove her forward, wanting to please him in a way that went to the very heart of who she was. And yet there was a hint of greed, wanting to make him need her in a way he'd never needed anyone else.

"Lindy…" Her name was groaned in a long stream that made her heart leap in her chest.

She leaned back and licked her lips with a slow smile.

Then he was pushing her backward, undoing her slacks and tugging them off in a quick motion that left no doubt as to what his intentions were. Her bra and lacy briefs followed in quick succession until he was leaning over her, kissing her mouth then letting his lips trail down the side of her jaw, nipping at her ear, suckling at her throat and then finally reaching one of her nipples and pulling hard. She arched off the bed, a storm tearing across her nerve endings as every part of her vied for his attention all at once. It was incredible. And she was quickly moving toward the point of no return. And when that happened, she wanted him inside her.

"Zeke." She breathed his name, her hand patting the area near her hip where he'd dropped the condom. He beat her to it, ripping open the packaging and rolling it down his length in one smooth movement. Seeing his hand on himself was heady and if they'd had the time she would have tried to explore that avenue a little bit more, but for now...

He parted her knees then reached beneath her hips to drag her toward the end of the bed. He lifted her toward him but then hovered there as if thinking.

She didn't want him thinking. She wanted him doing. Wrapping her legs around his ass, she let him know in no uncertain terms what she wanted. What she expected from him.

And then he was there, thrusting inside her with a quick move that took her breath away. He lowered her hips, following her down, and took her mouth even as he started to move. Her eyes fluttered closed, reveling in each and every sensation as it washed over her. He hadn't fully touched her, and yet she knew he wasn't going to need to. The friction of their bodies coming together was all the stimulation she needed as she pushed up, begging for more of the same.

When he changed the angle slightly, she gasped, eyes flicking back open to find him staring down at her. "Oh, God, Zeke, I've never…"

The heat in his gaze burned her alive. "Say my name again." He pushed hard inside her. "Say it."

"Zeke. Zeke… Zeke…"

He quickened his pace as she continued to whisper his name, hitting something with each thrust that made her nerve-endings burst into flame. Suddenly she was consumed in a rush that sent his name screaming from her lips, her body contracting around his. And then he was driving into her at a pace that seemed impossible before straining hard, every muscle in his face tense. Then he collapsed on top of her, his body rocking hers as tiny explosions continued to burst inside her.

Then it was over. His cheek slid against hers, and he rolled over, taking her with him. He kissed her. "What just happened here?"

The question took her aback, before she realized he wasn't really looking for an answer. He was just voicing the exact thing that she'd just thought.

And it was a good thing. Because she had no response to give him.

But the question repeated in her head. What just happened here?

And like his name during the height of passion, the question started getting louder and louder, until it was all she could hear.

She had to go to work and face this man

the day after tomorrow, and she suddenly wasn't sure she could. Not without him seeing the truth on her face. She'd meant this to be a one-time thing. A way to get him out of her head and off her mind. That plan had backfired, because right now he was all she could think about. Her new normal no longer felt so normal. She was jittery and unsure and starting to wonder if this had been such a good idea after all. She had no idea how to explain any of it to herself, much less to him.

"About Monday…" She couldn't find a single word that would get her meaning across. Especially not when she was lying on top of him, still enjoying the feeling of being connected to him.

He frowned. "What about it?"

And she heard it. A wariness in his voice that matched her thoughts and had her up and off him in an instant. He made no effort to get up and cover himself, but she sure as hell did, going into her bathroom and sliding into her robe.

When she went back into the bedroom he was sitting up, his hair sticking up in odd directions that gave him a boyish appearance that stopped at his eyes. They were old and weary, and held a resignation she'd never seen in him before.

Before she could try to assuage his fears and assure him that she didn't want things to change between them at work, he said, "I know this wasn't planned, on either of our parts, but it happened. As much as I enjoyed it, it can't change what happens in the operating room. Because if it does…if it interferes with our patients…" He took a long careful breath. "Then I don't want you there anymore."

He didn't want her there? Doing surgery with him? Or at the hospital itself.

"I'm not sure I understand."

He reached for her hand, catching it before she could pull away. "People put their lives in our hands. They trust us to have our minds fully on what needs to be done. If this changes that for either of us then we can't work together anymore."

A slice of pain went through her. Where she had just been going to say that she wanted things to be business as usual, he was saying he might not want to be associated with her at all now.

"Do…" Her voice caught, and she had to stop. Then fear was replaced with a bubble of anger. She had been about to ask him if he wanted her to quit, but that was something the old Lindy would have done when backed into a corner. The new Lindy had to grow a backbone or she would regret it. She changed the question to a statement. "I'm not quitting, if that's what you mean."

He stared at her for a second. "Hell, no. Where did you get that idea?"

"I just thought… You said we might not be able to work together anymore."

"I wasn't talking about the hospital in general." He dragged a hand through his hair and then got up. "Hold that thought for a minute."

He went into the bathroom with his briefs and when he re-emerged he was wearing them. "I don't know where you came up with that idea, but I would never ask you to quit. I just don't want what happened tonight to affect our patients. I feel I can put this into a compartment and keep it there during surgery. I hope you can too."

"Absolutely." He'd actually said what she'd been thinking much better than she could have. Relief washed over her. "It's not something that will happen again, so I vote that we just put it behind us."

"I concur." He looked a whole lot surer than she felt, but if he could adopt that certainty, she could too.

She really should thank him. It was much better to have had her first post-marriage sexual experience with someone that she instinctively trusted. Someone like Zeke.

Just thinking his name made her shiver. It had been exciting to know he liked hearing his name on her lips. And she liked hearing him call her Lind. Not many people called her that. Certainly never Luke, who'd never ever used a pet name for her. She'd liked it a little too much, and she needed to be careful not to infer anything from it.

Because what she'd said was true. She could fall for this man. Only he obviously had other ideas. Ideas that did not involve him and her together forever.

They were not a couple, and they were unlikely to ever become a couple, so she needed to get that thought right out of her head. They both needed to be on the same page about this. She didn't need to be mooning after him and wondering whether or not he felt the same. He didn't. He'd just said he could shove what had happened between them into a box and seal it up, probably for all eternity.

Lindy only hoped she was strong enough to do the same. She wasn't stupid. She knew that the feelings he'd generated in her tonight would easily turn into a form of infatuation if she wasn't careful. One that was based on nothing more than pleasurable sensations.

Pleasurable sensations? That was such a weak way of expressing how she'd felt. Which was part of the problem. She shouldn't be looking for stronger words.

She shook herself from her mental ramblings to see him standing there with his hands on his hips. Her heart skipped a beat. He was one of the most attractive men she'd ever laid eyes on. She needed him to get

dressed before she did something stupid.
Like peel those briefs off and haul him
back to bed. If that happened, it would be
a whole lot harder for her to let him go, or
compartmentalize what had happened, like
he wanted her to do.

"I'm glad we're in agreement on where to
go from here." She wasn't sure they were,
but that was all she could think of to say to
get him out of her bedroom and out of her
house.

As if reading her mind, he reached for
his slacks and pulled them on, one leg at a
time, buckling them around his waist. Realizing she was staring, she turned away and
tidied her bed and gathered her own clothes
before sitting on the edge of it. Except that
reminded her of the way she'd pulled him
toward her and slid her mouth…

Lord! She wasn't sure there was a compartment big enough to pack all of this away.
But she'd better find one, even if it meant
building it with her own two hands.

But at least he now had his clothes on, and
that wallet was tucked back in his pocket.
No fear of repeating what had happened.

At least not tonight, and hopefully not any other night. He'd already warned her. If she wanted any possibility of continuing to work with him, she'd better get her act together.

So she smiled and saw him to the door, and kept smiling as he walked toward his car and got in, leaving her with one of the worst cases of doubt she'd ever had.

Because as easy as it might be for Zeke to erase this from his memory, Lindy wasn't at all sure that she was going to be able to follow his example. But if she couldn't then she needed to pretend. And she'd better do a damned good job of it, or he was going to see right through it and straight into her heart.

CHAPTER EIGHT

ZEKE WAS GLAD to see Lindy already gowned and inside that operating room on Monday morning.

Even though she'd said she wanted to scrub in on Tessa's case, he hadn't been entirely sure she'd be there. Especially since he'd been so damned pompous about doing what was best for their patients. As if Lindy didn't feel the same way. He wouldn't have blamed her if she'd turned around and refused to work with him, and not because of what had happened the night before last. But because he'd acted like her boss and not her coworker.

Yes, she was a nurse, but that didn't mean he was higher than she was on the hiring chart. Yes, he might command the OR, but he didn't have the power to tell nurses where they could and couldn't work. Not without a good reason.

And he wasn't about to tell anyone what had happened between them.

He only hoped she could be just as tight-lipped. Not because he felt embarrassed or ashamed. He wasn't. But the workplace wasn't the best place to let these kinds of things play out. Things got twisted out of shape, and heaven forbid something went really wrong...

There it was again. That attitude that he was the only one who knew how to keep this contained. Lindy had just as much at stake as he did, if not more. She was new to the hospital. There was no way she'd want everyone to know that she'd slept with him. And he had no desire to hurt her career, or his own for that matter. So they would just do as he'd said and keep this between the two of them. Surely he was capable of that.

He gave her a smile that was a lot warmer than it should have been, but he was truly glad to see her. "Everything okay?"

"Yes, thank you." Her response was stilted and formal, but he could understand that. He hadn't meant to make her feel her job was in jeopardy, hadn't realized until afterward how she'd taken his words. He hoped he'd cleared that up, but maybe he hadn't entirely. But he wasn't sure at this point how to make his meaning any clearer.

Did he really think she couldn't keep her personal life and her professional life separate? No. The reality was that as he'd been lying on her bed, looking up at her, he had suddenly felt unsure whether or not *he* was going to be able to keep them separate. And that had terrified him.

There had been a sense of eager exploration on her part that had shocked him. As if the world before her was new and bright, waiting for her to go out and conquer it. It had hit him right between the eyes and moved him in a way that was alien to him.

He and his ex-wife had had a sexual relationship when they'd both been new to the game, but this had been different and new. Not that he had anything to compare it to. She was the first woman he'd been with since his divorce.

Maybe her reaction had stemmed from

her abuse. The fact that she trusted Zeke to *not* be that person touched him. It humbled him, but also made him realize that he was not the best person for her. He couldn't promise to be there when she needed him. After all, he'd proven once before that he wasn't trustworthy when it came to that. Instead of working through issues, he withdrew, resisting all efforts to reach him.

But he needed to get over that and be the professional he'd claimed he could be. So he took a deep breath.

"Ready, people?" He glanced around at the individuals in the room with him and saw the nods of those who had devoted themselves to the same cause that he had: saving lives and helping children live those lives in a way that gave them the best chance at happiness and wellness.

Unlike last time, when they'd used twilight sedation, Tessa was now under general anesthesia, since this surgery would be much more invasive than the last one. He'd already mapped out his plan for removing the tumor. It would involve taking out a piece of her stomach, but this particular organ was amazing in that it could stretch and adapt to the needs of the individual.

"Let's begin. Scalpel."

As in previous surgeries, Lindy anticipated his every need, placing the instrument in his gloved hand almost before he asked for it. Except this time, he was hyperaware of her fingers connecting with his. As much as he tried to tune it out, he couldn't. So he ignored it instead.

He found the tumor on the wall of Tessa's stomach and carefully clamped the blood supply to it. "Preparing to dissect." His hand was remarkably steady as he made his way around the border of the tumor, marking positions on a chart so that he could tell how the tumor had been situated. He would need that in case the pathology came back with tumor cells within the dissected edge. If he left cells behind, there was a good chance the tumor would grow back. Then he lifted it out and placed the growth in a stainless-steel basin that Lindy held up for him. "I need that taken to Pathology to see if the margins are clean."

One of the other nurses took the specimen container. "I'll be right back."

This was the waiting game. Pathology would do a quick scan to see if they could detect abnormal cells along the border, listing where they'd found them, if they did. If that happened, he would know exactly where to remove more tissue, which would then be rechecked.

There was no music. Zeke preferred to work in a quiet space, and his team knew that, keeping all conversations minimal and in low tones so as not to distract him. Lindy's eyes met his above the mask. "It looked good."

"Thank you." He glanced up at the anesthesiologist. "Everything okay?"

"She's in good shape."

The clocked ticked down the seconds and the sound seemed to ping in Zeke's head, time dragging out until it seemed almost a surreal dream. But it wasn't. This was a girl's life and he didn't want to close her without knowing it was safe to do so.

Ten minutes later the phone to the OR rang and one of the nurses picked it up. She looked at Zeke and gave him a thumbs-up sign then hung up. "All clear."

A series of pleased murmurs went through the room. "Let's close her up."

He sutured the stomach with small careful stitches, not wanting to risk a hole or a leak that could bring with it the danger of peritonitis and a second surgery or worse. As soon as he had that done, he sewed the abdominal muscles back in place and finally the layers of skin.

And then he was done. He glanced again at the clock. What he'd expected to take four hours had taken three. Part of that was due to the skill of his team, and specifically Lindy, who'd performed her duties brilliantly. He might have had a couple of rough patches, but she'd sailed through without a hitch.

"Good job as always, people. Let's wake her up. Anyone up for coffee?" He made sure he asked early enough that Lindy wouldn't feel put on the spot if no one else opted to go.

A couple of the other nurses indicated they could go and when he glanced at Lindy, she hesitated as if trying to decide where this fit in that whole personal versus professional discussion they'd had. Finally she nodded.

Relief washed through him like a flood. Maybe they were going to be able to get through this after all. Or at least he was. Maybe she'd misread his intentions as much as he'd thought she had. Or at least was willing to give him the benefit of the doubt.

And sometimes that was all he could ask. But from now on, no more movie nights with Lindy and her daughter, and no more nights of any kind with Lindy. For his own peace of mind.

Daisy ran down the hospital corridor and latched onto his leg before he could back away. Zeke stood stock still before looking down at the tyke who'd attached herself to him. Marina used to run up to him and do exactly the same thing, looking up at him with her sweet smile.

But this wasn't his daughter. And she never would be.

Lindy hurried down the corridor and

caught up with Daisy. "I'm so sorry. I didn't realize she'd slipped away from me until it was too late."

He swallowed. The same could be said of Marina. He hadn't realized she'd slipped away either, until it had been too late. And realizing she was never coming back again had taken even longer to sink in. And when it had...

Clenching his jaw, he forced a smile that probably looked as ghastly as it felt. "It's fine."

"Daisy, you need to let go of him." She pried the child's fingers loose and then swung her up into her arms.

Daisy looked right at him. "Can Zeke come?"

"No, not tonight."

That's right. It was Friday night. A full week since the last disastrous one, when he'd taken Lindy home and made love to her.

She hadn't asked him to come. In fact, she'd made it clear she didn't want him to. It was good, because that way he wouldn't have to turn down the invitation. Which he would have. Right?

"What's the film?" he asked out of curiosity, not because he was going.

"*Princess Diaries*!" Daisy's answer was immediate, the delight in her face obvious.

He couldn't hold back his grin. "You still like princesses, huh?"

"Princess!"

When he glanced at Lindy, her face was tense. "Don't worry. I won't come."

"I didn't mean..."

"I know you didn't."

Even so, she seemed to hug Daisy tighter as if closing him out of their little circle. That stung, and he got his first whiff of what it was like to be shut out. "I don't want my parents to get any funny ideas, which they might if it became a regular thing."

His brows went up. The thought of movie night and all that went with it becoming a regular thing made something inside him perk up. He quickly put it right back in its place. Not only because of work but because of how right it felt having Daisy cling to him.

"I don't want them to get any funny ideas either." He forced himself to give Daisy's nose a light-hearted tweak. "Even though I'll miss the princesses."

Realizing how that sounded, he added, "The ones on the screen."

Well, that didn't make it much better. He seemed determined to make a mess of things, even when trying to straighten them out. All the more reason to leave things where they'd left them.

Daisy laughed and hugged her mom tight before giving a loud wheezing cough.

His chest gave a sudden squeeze. "Is she okay?"

"Yes, just an allergy or something. She gets them periodically."

An allergy. Or something. Hadn't he said those very words?

"Have you had it checked out?"

Lindy looked up at him with a sideways grin. "I'm a nurse, remember? Yes. I checked her out. And I had her pediatrician check her out. Nothing to worry about."

A few of his muscles relaxed, even though he'd been a doctor at the time that Marina had fallen ill and had missed the signs. Another reminder of why getting involved with someone with a child was not a good idea.

He was happy the way he was, his job giving him all the love and fulfillment he needed.

At least that's what he had told himself time and time again.

Was he starting to doubt that?

Maybe he was, because he felt a little flat, knowing he wasn't going to be spending the evening in the company of Daisy and her mother.

Lindy was evidently a whole lot better at compartmentalizing than he was.

"Well, I'm glad she's okay."

"Speaking of okay…" she shifted Daisy a little higher on her hip "…how is Tessa doing? I heard that her parents were really happy about the outcome of her surgery. Any idea when she'll be discharged? I'm assuming she'll still be here tomorrow. I was hoping to run by and see her, if so."

"She won't be discharged for another day or two. I want to make sure her system reboots itself once we introduce liquids and solids back into her diet. And, yes, her parents consider themselves very lucky."

"I'm sure they do. You're a great surgeon."

He hadn't meant about that. "No, they feel very lucky that the tumor was benign." He understood the relief they must have felt, even if he hadn't experienced that first-hand.

"I'm pretty sure they feel lucky to have had you operating on her too. Don't sell yourself short."

"I'm not." He knew he was a good surgeon. But he sometimes wondered if he was lacking in the empathy department, trying to keep himself emotionally removed from his patients even as he tried his best to save them. The same way he'd kept his wife at arm's length at times. Tessa had somehow broken through that barrier, at least on some level. And Daisy had wormed her way in even further. He was going to have to be careful or pretty soon he wasn't going to have any wall of protection left.

Did he even really need one?

He used to think he did. And now?

"Well, we'd better go. Mom went down

to visit a sick friend and was going to meet us back in the lobby."

"Have a good time tonight. At least you'll get to bed at a decent hour." He couldn't resist that little rejoinder. The sudden pink tinge to her face said she knew exactly what he was referring to.

"Well, I guess you will too."

That was doubtful at this point, but he wasn't about to tell her that he'd spent a few sleepless nights remembering what they'd done a week ago. And talking about it, even in a half-teasing way, wasn't going to help him in that area. Better to just drop the subject before it got any deeper. Or he changed his mind about coming to watch Daisy's latest princess movie.

Because the further he steered away from any thoughts of an after-party, the better.

Three days later, Lindy and Zeke were parked outside a neighboring hospital, where they were going to see if its helpline project would fit in with what Mid Savannah wanted to do with a women's center. They were to spend a couple of hours there and then report back to Neil and the committee later in the week. The idea was to jump in and see how things ran.

And if it came to actually answering phones?

Lindy wasn't sure she could bare her soul to a complete stranger. But she'd done it at her other volunteer job, and these were strangers who needed help. And hadn't she bared her soul to Zeke when he'd been practically a stranger? She had, and she was none the worse for wear. Not from that anyway.

Taking a deep breath, she waited for Zeke to push through the door and followed him in. They found the place empty except for two people—one of whom was seated at a desk, a phone in her hand, and the other person, who looked to be a supervisor, was leaning over her. The man scribbled something on a pad of paper and pushed it toward the person on the phone. Lindy's misgivings grew. Was that person on a tough call? She had no way of knowing.

The man motioned them over, where they waited for him to finish helping the volunteer.

The small office looked like it had actually been a large supply closet at one time, so there wasn't room for an army of people all talking at once. As it was, it was a little cramped with just the four of them.

She'd been thinking more along the lines of something bigger. With room for two or three people working at one time. And the ability to take walk-ins off the street if it came down to it.

But one volunteer? There would be no one to pass the client to if whoever was on duty got in over their head or landed in a dangerous situation.

No. That wasn't entirely true. When Lindy had spoken with the person in charge of the service she'd been told they could get on another line and either call 911 or get in touch with one of the agencies that dealt with issues that were more complicated. Or more dangerous. That was a good point to remember when they opened their clinic. The place she used to volunteer at had a panic button that would notify the police in case an irate partner came in. A button she'd never had to push, thank God.

She glanced at Zeke and said in hushed tones, "Have you been here before?"

"No, first time, and I have to tell you this isn't what I had in mind."

"Me neither. The place I worked at had multiple lines and a place where people who were in trouble came to get help."

She went on. "I do have a line on a building that I want to check out after we leave here." She'd felt horrible calling Zeke in on his day off, especially for what had turned out to be such a small operation, but Neil had been getting pressure from some of his board who wanted to see them move on this thing quickly.

Quick didn't always equal better.

She moved toward the pair who were working together on the phone and overheard the other volunteer trying to get an address. The phone was on speaker and the woman on the other end seemed angry.

"I just want to know where I can find a good lawyer to sue my boyfriend. Like I said, he hit me."

The caller's voice sounded belligerent rather than frightened and for Lindy, that sent up an automatic red flag.

"I can't do that, but I can get you some

help, if you're in danger. What is your boy-friend's name?"

"I'm not saying." A few choice words came over the speaker, causing the volunteer to glance up at her supervisor with raised brows.

It was then that Lindy saw what he'd writ-ten on the pad.

Possible hoax.

It did sound like it and the person's speech sounded almost slurred, as if she'd been drinking or was taking something that im-paired her thinking. "Then can you give me your address so that we can make sure you're safe?"

Click.

The caller had hung up. The volunteer sighed. Young, with long blond hair and baby-blue eyes, she introduced herself as Tara Sanders.

"Sorry to have called you in here for noth-ing," she said to the man, who introduced himself as Todd Grissom. "I've just never had a caller like that before. I thought she was suicidal at first. She didn't ask for a lawyer until just a second ago."

Todd glanced at them. "We find it's better to give people the benefit of the doubt, when possible. But as she hung up, our hands are tied. We can hand the recording over to the police department and see if there's anything in there they can use, and of course we'll keep a record of the cellphone number, just like we do with all our calls."

Zeke glanced around. "I see another desk and a phone." He nodded behind the current volunteer.

"We do have another line. Unfortunately, we don't have enough volunteers to man it. We're probably going to throw in the towel if nothing changes in the next couple of months."

Lindy didn't understand. "Were there enough volunteers when your program started up?"

This time it was Tara who answered. "I've been volunteering for three years and we used to have a lot of people. But people get tired, you know? Burned out. It seems like there's a never-ending stream of people who need help and not enough resources to go around."

Which was exactly why Mid Savannah was interested in opening their own center. Neil said they'd had a plea from another organization saying an actual medical-based facility was needed. People could always come to the hospital, but the tangles of insurance and red tape sometimes kept them from trying to get help. They wanted an actual place with an exam room or two, along with a place to conduct group sessions or one-on-one counseling. The phones would be used as a filter and a way to direct folks to the right place on the right day.

"How many callers would you say you log in an average day?" she asked.

"You mean on this phone or both of them together?"

"Let's say both of them." Even as she said it the phone behind Tara began to ring. Todd went back to get that one, speaking in low tones as he jotted down what the caller said.

"I'd say we get around forty calls in a day."

"So in an eight-hour period there are

around five calls an hour." Less than fifteen minutes per caller. "And if someone calls while you're on the line?"

"They'll get a busy signal. Todd only answers if there's no one else available. He knows how hard it can be for some of them to confide in a man. But there are no guarantees the caller will try again later."

"They'll get a busy signal."

Lindy had visions of their lobby flooded with people and not enough bodies to handle them "Great. Thanks so much for letting us come and observe."

"Do you want to try taking a call? We have a book with prompts that help a lot. You told me you volunteered at Gretchen's Place, didn't you?"

"I did."

"Did you do phone work?"

"Yes. It was pretty busy as well."

The difference had been that their volunteers hadn't petered out.

Tara reached under her desk and hefted a large three-ring binder, setting it on the desk.

Okay, wow, that was bigger than anything

they'd had at Gretchen's Place. "How do you find anything in there?"

"It's all alphabetized."

Todd was still in the background on the phone. It sounded like he was trying to get someone to turn himself in.

Lindy glanced at Zeke. "We'll go as soon as I try this, okay? Unless you want a turn as well."

Zeke shook his head. "I do better in person than on the phone."

She certainly understood that. Was that true? Or was he quickly realizing this was going to be more involved than simply empathizing with at-risk women and trying to get them help, the way she herself had once needed help?

"Gretchen's Place had a log that we entered all calls into."

Tara flipped to the first page of the binder. "We have that as well. And you'll need to record the call and notify the person on the other end that you're doing so. You'll assign the recording the next number in the sequence. Doing that will automatically save it to the computer, and we can retrieve it at a later date along with the actual recording and time stamp. It helps us cover ourselves in the event that someone challenges our version of a conversation."

She was impressed. From her initial impression and the tiny size of the office, Lindy hadn't expected the helpline to be as sophisticated as it was, but it sounded like they'd started off well and things had just fizzled out, for whatever reason. It was a good reminder that you couldn't grow complacent about the mission or it would lose its momentum.

She'd never known Mid Savannah Medical Center to do things in half-measures. Not that she'd been there all that long, but from everything she'd seen, they liked to stay on top of things. The hospital she'd worked at before her marriage had also paid attention to the little things, but it had been a much smaller facility and it was doubtful they would have had the resources to open up a place even as small as this one.

And somehow she couldn't imagine her and Zeke trapped in a tiny cubicle for two or three hours. His lanky figure already ate up a great deal of the available air space. And he was rapidly taking up a great deal of her thoughts as well. He'd once said he couldn't work with her if she couldn't maintain that separation of professional and personal. Well, it was hard enough in their huge hospital. In here, it would be impossible.

Friday night movies hadn't been quite the same without him, however, and her mom had insisted on keeping a sleeping Daisy for the night yesterday. If only she'd done that the Friday before, maybe she and Zeke would have never had their encounter. Except she had enjoyed her time with him, was glad for it no matter what else happened.

She glanced at Tara. "Anything of crucial importance inside that book?" Maybe she could treat it like her other hospital's helpline. Surely it couldn't be all that different.

She slid into the chair and looked at the open screen on the desk. Tara grabbed a second chair and sat beside her. "There is, but you won't have to deal with most of it." The other woman flipped a couple of tabs and opened the page to a list of phone numbers.

"These are the organizations that you'll want to keep track of. They're also on one of the screens."

She leaned across and clicked an icon labeled "Resource Referrals." A page identical to the one in the binder popped onto the screen. "It's here, so the book doesn't have to be pulled out every time we want to give someone a phone number. And of course 911 is exactly the same."

Tara continued. "Mostly you want to listen and make sure the caller isn't in immediate danger, like we said earlier."

"If I suspect someone is in danger, even if the caller claims she isn't, can I still call and report it?"

"Absolutely. That's happened more than once, and we'd much rather be on the safe side than risk someone's life."

"Once you disconnect, the computer will ask you if you want to save or delete. You'll always want to save. Periodically, one of the other board members will go through calls that were marked non-urgent and cross-reference them to other calls. If it was a one-off and there was a satisfactory resolution, such as finding the appropriate place to send her, then we'll delete the actual recording to free up space. But the phone number and time stamp will remain to help with writing grant requests."

"Okay, got it."

She glanced up and caught Zeke's eyes on her. Damn! How was she going to concentrate on a caller when he was looking at her like that?

Like what?

She wasn't sure. But she liked it.

Their night together almost seemed like a dream now, a surreal combination of physical and emotional reactions that could have belonged to someone else. Only they didn't. They belonged to her and she did not want to give them up. Not yet.

That sexy mouth went up in a half-smile that made her stomach flip.

"What?"

"Nothing. Just anxious to see you in action."

She gave him a sharp look, but there was nothing there to indicate the words had any other meaning.

Was she the only one having trouble wiping those memories from her skull? If only it was as easy to zap them away as it was to erase the call files from the computer. But like Tara said, even if that happened, there would probably still be some kind of record, a mental paper trail that would remain with her forever.

And that's probably the way it should be. Every experience in life brought an opportunity to learn and grow. Though she wasn't quite sure what she'd learned from that night other than to be more careful about letting her sexual urges run amok.

That made her smile, because it perfectly described what had happened. She'd let them out for the first time in ages and they'd gone a little wild and crazy on her.

Wild and crazy. Like her toenail polish. She remembered using those words. Remembered him saying them back to her. As if he knew exactly what she was thinking about, his dark eyes dropped to her mouth for a brief second before swiftly returning to her face as a whole.

Tara cocked her head. "Something funny?"

Somehow her smile had frozen in place. She wiped it away as quickly as she could. She needed to get control of herself. "No, sorry. What else do I need to know?"

Instead of Tara answering, it was Zeke. "You already know enough to get you into a whole lot of trouble. I don't think you need to know any more."

Um, what kind of trouble was he talking about?

Her mind had swung onto a detour. And he knew it. Knew what he'd done to her with those few simple words.

Tara smiled. "He's right. There's no reason to try to stuff everything in your head for one caller."

She was right. About the helpline. And about the other stuff?

What she would like to do was admit that she wanted his mouth back on hers. But that wasn't going to happen. Not now. Maybe not ever again.

The phone suddenly rang, making her jump. Oh, Lord, could she really do this?

Tara rubbed her hands together. "Okay. It's showtime. I'll be right here if you need me."

Unfortunately, it wasn't Tara she needed. It was Zeke. And she was very afraid that he already knew exactly how he affected her. And that there was no way in heaven or on earth that she could let him know. Because Zeke wasn't offering a lifetime. He wasn't even offering to repeat their last encounter. So she picked up the phone and gave a shaky greeting and waited to see who was on the other end of the line.

CHAPTER NINE

Somehow Zeke got through the next two hours of visiting the call center and then a building a few blocks away. It had been one thing to be cramped in a tiny space when there'd been other people around, but to be standing in a large open warehouse with no one but a realtor, who politely waited outside while they looked around, was much worse.

At the call center he'd been a brave man teasing her when he'd known they could do nothing about it. But he'd sensed her wound so tightly in there that he'd been afraid she might burst.

Afraid to be back in that world where there was fear and denial. So he'd tried to lighten the atmosphere and had ended up almost setting himself on fire in the process.

He had a feeling that he and Lindy had

something in common besides a single night of sex. And it wasn't nearly as fun.

Could she have PTSD from her experience? Of course she could. Just as any of them could from a deep-seated trauma. Including him.

That sex, though, had blotted out everything for a brief period of time. It had been like an addictive drug that when used once hooked the user for the rest of his life. Zeke already found himself wanting more. Only they'd both agreed that wasn't happening.

She finally finished looking at the building. "Well, I think this one's a possibility."

"A lot of money to revamp it to fit our purposes, though."

"I think anything will be."

They got back into her car and she switched on the ignition.

Touching her shoulder, he swiveled in his seat to face her. "Are you okay?"

"I think so. I'm pretty keyed up right now, though. I probably won't be able to sleep for a while. Do you want me to drop you off at home or at the hospital?"

Since it was only seven o'clock, he doubted

she would go home and hop right into bed. Besides, she had Daisy to deal with, unless she was sleeping over at Rachel and Harold's tonight.

"Do you have to pick up Daisy?"

"No, Mom is keeping her."

"Good. It probably would be a good idea for you to unwind."

"After sitting for the last two hours? I feel like I need to be up doing something. I need to burn off some energy."

It wouldn't be dark for a while, and he didn't really feel like going home to an empty house either. But what else could he do? Just then he saw a poster hanging on a street sign. It was the perfect solution. "I don't know if you're up for it, but Savannah hosts a jazz festival every year. I just saw a sign for it. I'm pretty sure tonight's is in Forsythe Park. It's probably partway over, but it's free, if you're interested. Otherwise drop me off at the hospital so I can get my car."

"I remember those, although it's been ages since I've been to one. You're thinking of going?"

"I thought I might. Care to join me?"

Zeke wasn't quite ready to go home, and the thought of going to the concert by himself was depressing.

He'd given up on finding Marina's age progression pictures but, then again, he hadn't really tried. He kept putting it off. And maybe that's what asking her to a concert was about as well. But sitting on a blanket listening to live music appealed to him. Like Lindy, it had been ages since he'd gone to one of the events, and tonight seemed like the perfect night. It would give the rapid firing of neurons in his head a chance to slow their pace.

And music? The perfect stress reliever. Well, almost perfect. The only thing better would have been…

Nope, not going there. He was going to have to find his endorphin fix in a different place.

"The jazz festival sounds perfect. I think I have a blanket in the back of my car from when I took Daisy on a picnic after we moved back, if you don't mind sitting on the ground."

With her? That sounded like heaven, and

he still wasn't sure why. Maybe the snatches of memories from their night together were holding him enthralled. Well, that would diminish with time. Maybe if he was with her in a non-sexual way, his body would get used to the idea that he wasn't going back to visit again, that it was firmly part of his past.

Like his ex. And Marina.

A bucket of pain sloshed over him, but he ignored it, pulling out his phone and saying, "I can't think of a better way to listen to one of those concerts. Let me just check to make sure it's at the park and not the theater." The concerts were sometimes split between the two venues. If it was inside, seating was limited. Scrolling down until he found today's date, he nodded. "It's at the park."

"Great. That settles it, then. Do you want me to drive?"

He smiled, his heart suddenly light. "How about you provide the seating, and I'll provide the transportation? Does that sound like a semi-equitable trade?"

Within five minutes they were on their way in his car, her blanket folded on the backseat. He was glad she'd agreed to come, the tiredness of mind and body dissipating almost immediately and warm anticipation taking its place. As hot and humid as it was in the summer and early fall, September was the beginning of a modicum of relief from the constant heat. And right now, with the sun starting to descend, the weather was comfortably balmy, if not cool.

Finding a place to park proved to be a bit of a challenge, since they'd arrived after things had already started. The plaintive sound of a saxophone reached them, even through the closed windows of his Jaguar, the one real luxury item he'd allowed himself.

Pulling the blanket from Lindy's more sensible car had made something inside him warm. He had imagined her and Daisy having conversations as they drove to the store or to Rachel and Harold's place. It had set up an ache in him that he'd tried to banish but he hadn't been entirely successful. He'd pushed it back, but it was there hovering in the background, waiting for another opportunity to make itself known. It actually would have been nice to bring Daisy out here, the three of them sitting together.

The ache took a step forward, but Zeke clenched his jaw and it retreated once again.

There! Someone was pulling out of a spot. Just in time. He slid into the space and shut the car off.

"This is great. Thanks for thinking of it. I wasn't looking forward to going home to an empty house but didn't want to admit that to my mom when she suggested she keep Daisy for the night."

"That makes two of us. The thought of sitting at home staring at the walls didn't appeal to me either. So we'll enjoy some good music and even better company."

They got out of the car and he retrieved the blanket. Lindy's light floral scent clung to the fabric. Folding it over his arm set the scent free, and he breathed deeply. He almost said the words "Next time..." but somehow called them back before they left his throat.

Why would there be a next time? He might have coffee with her periodically after a shared surgery, but he wouldn't be sitting in the office of the women's center week after week. He didn't have time to, first and foremost, and secondly he was pretty sure that Lindy would find it odd if he somehow managed to appear each and every time she volunteered. So he'd better take advantage of tonight and enjoy himself. Because he wasn't sure when he would get the chance to do something like this again.

They wove their way between people, and Zeke glanced at the stage periodically. The saxophone was still playing, the light notes spiraling from the stage to their intended target, his ears absorbing the sound.

There they went…those muscles in his neck. They were starting to soften and relax, and his headache began to ease.

"How's this?" He'd found a spot big enough to toss open the blanket without hitting anyone and where they wouldn't feel like they were sitting on top of those surrounding them.

"Perfect."

Zeke shook it open and spread it on the ground, waiting while she kicked off her shoes and eased her way down, knees bent, arms wrapped around them. She arched her neck way back, while tilting her head to the right and left as if she had a few kinks of her own to get rid of. Her dark hair touched the blanket behind her, sliding back and forth as she continued to work at it.

"Sore?"

"A little. I'm not sure why."

Maybe the music had lulled him into a false sense of security, because when her hand went to her nape, as if trying to tackle the ache on her own, he couldn't resist.

"Here, let me." He toed off his loafers and sat beside her, one hand sliding under her hair and massaging the muscles he found there with firm strokes.

"Mmm, that feels good, thanks."

Focusing on the stage, he let the music wash over him as he kept ministering to her nape and the sides of her neck, his thumb gliding up and down her soft skin.

When he glanced over at her, her eyes were closed, but she wasn't sleeping. What he hoped she was doing was enjoying the feel of his fingers pressing deep into her tight muscles and loosening them up, one

section at a time. What he was doing probably wasn't obvious to anyone around them
and even if it was, it wasn't any different
from what any man might do for someone
he loved.

Only he didn't love her. He needed to remember that. So what *were* his feelings toward her?

Hell if he knew. But one thing was for
sure. The feelings weren't platonic. No matter how many times he might lecture himself or how many examples of friendship
he might hold up, he knew there had to be
a third option. Something he hadn't quite
reached or achieved. Some deep transcen-
dental realm that he needed to find.

As if reading his mind, she took a deep
breath and let it out on a sigh before leaning to the side slightly. "Thanks. I'm good."
She stretched her legs out in front of her
and leaned back on her elbows. The polish
on her toes had changed. The glittery silver
had been replaced by some kind of opales-
cent purple that seemed to shift colors each
time she moved her feet, which she was now

doing, one foot moving sideways, keeping time with the beat.

"More wild and crazy?"

She glanced at him and then looked at her feet and laughed. "Oh, yes. Everyone should have at least one wild and crazy side."

He'd been the recipient of another wild and crazy side, then shut that line of thought down. They were here for the music and nothing else.

Planting his hands on the blanket behind him, he forced himself to settle and relax as the quick notes continued to dance around them. Low conversations were taking place as dusk enfolded them in shadows, and as he looked, he saw all types of people, some on lawn chairs, some on blankets like they were, and some simply sitting on the grassy expanse. But one thing they all had in common was a love of a way of life that was both old and new. Savannah had a charm that he hadn't found in many other places.

And Lindy fit right into that charm. Being away from her hometown hadn't killed it, although there was a solemnity to that wild and crazy side that had probably come from what she'd endured.

As it had a couple of times before, anger rolled up his gut. How could any man do such damage to someone he was supposed to love? And worse, not care whether or not his child was around while it was happening. Thank God, Daisy had been an infant at the time. He could not imagine his daughter seeing such an ugly side of human nature, and Zeke had a hard time understanding what could generate so much rage that someone would lash out at another person.

He wouldn't. And most people he knew wouldn't, although he did know that abusers could come across as great people when you met them on the street or worked with them. It was only those at home who saw the truth.

That was the dangerous side to compartmentalizing, the very thing he'd told himself he needed to do in regard to the night he and Lindy had spent together. But making love hadn't hurt anyone. Except maybe his "want to," which he now kept locked up.

And that guy needed to stay there. At least when Lindy was around.

So he settled in to enjoy this side of being with her. And actually he had probably seen Lindy in more settings than he had any other woman at the hospital. He'd seen worried Lindy, competent Lindy, concerned Lindy... and sexy-as-hell Lindy. And those facets were all rolled into one fascinating woman. It was no wonder he wanted her.

And she'd wanted him. At least she had for one night.

"He's so good." A soft voice came from beside him and he tensed at first, confused as to what she was saying, then he realized she was referring to the musician.

What had he thought? That she was muttering something about him under her breath? Not very likely.

"Yes, he is. I don't think I've heard him before but, like I said, it's been years since I've been to one of the festivals. He might have been in diapers the last time I came."

She gave a light laugh. "You're not quite that ancient. If he was in diapers, then you probably were too. He can't be any older than thirty-five or -six."

"How did you guess my age?"

"You have that look about you."

That made him frown. "What kind of look is that?" It didn't sound exactly flattering to hear her say that.

"That crinkling around your eyes from laughter."

"So I have wrinkles, do I?"

"Not wrinkles. Crinkles. There's a big difference."

He suddenly found himself wanting to know exactly what that difference was. "Explain it to me."

"Wrinkles are caused by worry or stress. Crinkles are caused by happiness."

They were? He didn't normally feel happy. But maybe she saw a side to him that he'd missed. His job made him happy. Could that actually express itself in the way lines were woven into the fabric of someone's skin? Maybe.

"You have crinkles too."

"I do? Where?"

He leaned over and touched a finger to the

bridge of her nose and let it slide down the side nearest him. "Here. When you smile, the skin here crinkles. I remember the first time I saw them."

"Really?"

"Yes. You were in the operating room and you had your surgical mask on. I could tell whether or not you were smiling by the lines—or lack thereof—on either side of your nose. It was damned attractive."

"Wow. I didn't know. And I certainly can't imagine that looking good. To anyone."

"Well, it does." He had no idea why he was admitting any of this, except that she'd brought up the subject by explaining what she thought so-called crinkles represented. He liked her thinking of him as being happy. He couldn't remember the last time someone had said that of him, even his mom, who was carrying some long-term grief herself over the death of her husband of thirty-four years. Marina and his dad had died within a few years of each other. He guessed it really was true. Grief had no expiration date.

Or maybe it could have. If he let it.

What exactly was the problem with him and Lindy being together? He'd made it into such a big thing in his head, but maybe it wasn't. As long as she didn't want promises of forever—which she'd never even implied she did—and probably didn't honestly, after what she'd been through. But maybe being with her had caused some of his wrinkles to make the shift into crinkles.

Or maybe he'd been generating them all along. But suddenly he thought that coming to the concert was the stupidest idea he could have come up with. Why hadn't he just taken her back to his place and done what he really wanted to do?

Was it because of the whole "bad idea" thing? Or was it because he'd thought she might reject him? Maybe it was a little of both, but he was about to test one of those theories. Whether the other was tested or not depended on her response.

"Lind, how interested are you in staying for the entire concert?"

That got her attention. Her eyes met his and she seemed to look at him forever, although it was probably only a few seconds.

Then she smiled...and there they were: crinkles. On either side of her nose. "I think I could be talked into slipping out a little early."

He leaned over the blanket and gave her a gentle kiss. It was the only way he could think of to make his intentions known. And when she curled her fingers around his neck and held him there for a second, he had his answer. He stood, reaching a hand down to help her up and then whipping the blanket back over his arm. There were some looks of confusion from those around them, but a couple of other folks knew exactly what was going on. After all, jazz's smooth, silky notes made it the perfect intro for what was on his mind. From the moment he'd suggested coming here, things had been moving in this direction, only he'd been too stupid— or maybe too smart—to admit it to himself.

And now he didn't care.

He tossed the blanket into the back of his car. The second they were in the car his lips were on hers and it was all he could do to pull away from her and put the car in gear. He didn't want to take the time to go all the way back home, wanted to do it right here in this car. But it was very probable they'd be arrested before they got to the best stuff. And that was definitely not the stuff crinkles were made of. So he added gas and eased off the clutch and headed back the way they'd come.

His apartment was on the far side of town and it took them almost a half-hour to get there. The whole time Lindy's palm had been splayed across his right thigh, and with each shift of gears, each time his foot came off the gas pedal, it seemed to slip a little bit higher. He wasn't quite sure if he was causing it or if she was purposely moving her hand. Whatever it was, he was hot and hard and was having a godawful time concentrating on the road in front of him.

But he'd better, or they were going to crash into one of the posts along the highway, and if he survived, he'd have to explain to law enforcement exactly why he'd been driving while distracted. He didn't think Lindy's parents would approve of him putting their daughter in the hospital. So although it took a monumental effort, he glanced over at her. "You go much higher with that hand and I'm going to have to pull off the road and find a bank of trees to hide away in."

"Would that be so bad?"

"No." He laughed. "Not bad at all, but I'd rather have you in bed, where I can do anything I want to you."

Her hand edged higher. "Does that mean I can do anything I want to you too?"

"Yes, baby, you can do absolutely anything your heart desires."

And there went that hand yet again. He gritted his teeth and prayed for mercy.

They hit what must have been Zeke's apartment door with a rattle of keys and her back pressed against the solid surface as he kissed her again and again. She never would have believed she could be so turned on by a car ride where they'd barely touched, but anything and everything had been implied, even without saying it outright.

His pelvis pressed into her in the deserted corridor as he tried to fit his key into the lock beside her. She laughed and slid sideways to let him have better access.

To the lock. And to certain regions of her body that were hoping to get a little satisfaction. The door swung open without warning and she careened backward, only just barely missing falling by him grabbing hold of her wrist. That didn't stop her from knocking over a bookshelf that was next to the door. Papers and framed awards sprayed in every direction. She gave a horrified murmur and turned to clean up the mess.

"Leave it." He was still holding her hand, coming up behind her and turning her to face him. "They're just things, Lind. Nothing to worry about."

God. She wanted this man. Wrapping her arms around his neck, she went up on tiptoe. "In that case, we're either going to spend some time on the long leather sofa that I see on my right or you're going to take me to your bedroom and show me exactly what you meant earlier when you said I could do anything I wanted."

He bit her lip. "Did I say anything? That term might have been a little too sweeping."

"Uh-uh. No give-backs."

"Maybe you'd better tell me what you have in mind, then."

He leaned his head down and in a sudden boost of confidence she whispered the naughtiest thing she could think of in his ear. The thing she'd thought about last time as he'd rolled his condom over his length.

His answering laugh was rough-edged with what sounded like disbelief. "I'm pretty sure that's not going to happen. I don't intend this to be a party of one."

"But you promised…" Talking like this, freely, without shame, was the biggest turn-on of all. She couldn't wait to get this man in bed and feel him in her, over her. Once had definitely not been enough. Especially since there was some kind of raw emotion twisting its way out of her. Something that made her look at him—at everything that made Zeke who he was. And it was just…

God. Oh, *God*! She loved him.

Loved him. Loved his laugh. Loved his crinkles. Loved his wrinkles, even. Loved the way he made her feel.

How was this even possible? She didn't

know, but she gloried in realizing it was possible to feel something profound. Something that felt sacred and good. And whether it worked out or not, she owed Zeke a debt of gratitude, and she intended to start paying it now.

She didn't have to wait for the bedroom. The party could start right here. Right now. With hurried hands, she reached for his belt and undid it, and the button of his slacks, then his zipper. She was wild for him, wanted him to take her now, as all the foreplay she'd needed had happened on the way over here: in the car, in the elevator, at his front door.

Then she had him out, his hard length in her hands, glorying in the heat coming off his skin, in the hiss of his breath as she tightened her fingers around him and pumped.

"God, Lindy." He cupped her face. "What are you doing to me?"

"If you won't do it, someone has to." She stretched up and bit his lip. Hard, letting him know she was not afraid of rough, because she knew he wouldn't hurt her. Not really.

She let go of him long enough to push her own slacks down her hips, her undergarments following quickly. She needed him. Right now. They could slow it down later.

Zeke got the idea and eased her down to the floor, making short work of finding a condom and sheathing himself. But this time, instead of thrusting into her, he rolled over so that she was on top, the way they'd ended the last time. Only this time they were just beginning. Just getting started.

She lowered herself onto him, that luscious sense of fullness so very perfect. Just like him. He took hold of her hips, but instead of guiding her, he let her set the rhythm, simply gripping her as she took him all the way in and then lifted off him.

Closing her eyes, she concentrated on the sensations that were washing over her and slowly building. She picked up the pace, vaguely hearing him mutter something under his breath. Whatever it was, it sounded like he approved. Her world was spinning in on itself, becoming denser and more compressed the faster it whirled. Her hands went to his shoulders, using his body as leverage as she rose up and came down again and again, the feeling of power it gave her heady. Her movements sped up as she got closer and closer to the zenith, a searing heat growing in her belly. And then it hit. Hard and long, her brain losing its ability to process for a second or two. Zeke shouted beneath her as he followed her into oblivion.

An oblivion that was more beautiful than anything she'd ever experienced.

She loved him. God. She couldn't get enough of those words, wanted desperately to say them aloud, but she didn't dare, clenching her teeth around them and keeping them inside.

Then it was over. She pulled in a breath and then another, her fingers reaching to sift through his hair. And then he opened those gorgeous brown eyes of his, and she was lost all over again.

"That was...incredible." He reached up and cupped the back of her head, tugging her down for a kiss. And then another. "I can't seem to get enough of you."

"I think you just did."

One side of his mouth went up in a smile.

"You only think I did. But that was your turn. And now it's mine."

Then he turned onto his side, dumping her off him. "Hey!" Her brief attempt at a protest ended in a laugh as he climbed to his feet and reached down a hand.

"This time we're going to bed. You don't have to go home, and I already am home, so you're going to spend the night."

He didn't ask, which made her smile. "What makes you think I'll say yes?"

"Remember that thing you wanted me to do? The one I said no to?"

A spark ignited in her belly. "Are you saying…?"

His smile grew. "Tell me you'll spend the night, and you'll find out."

"I'll spend the night. Gladly." He didn't have to coax her. She would have stayed even without the hinted promise.

"Then, my dear, you're about to get your wish. And I'm about to get mine." With that he led her through to the bedroom and shut the door behind them.

CHAPTER TEN

ZEKE WOKE UP in a swirl of confusion, unsure of where he was. For a panicked second, he thought he'd forgotten to go to work before realizing it was still early. He glanced at the readout on his phone. Barely six.

He heard some kind of scraping noise, like furniture being dragged across the floor, and tensed before the events of the previous night came flooding back.

Lindy had stayed with him and they'd made love… He tried to count and failed. The events were pretty much a blur. Except for the fact that his muscles were loose and relaxed, so much so that he wasn't sure they were going to let him get up.

But where was Lindy?

Had she left?

He frowned before hearing the same

sound he'd noticed a second ago, a little louder this time.

That had to be her. But what was she doing? Trying to leave before he woke up?

He didn't like that. Last night, just before he'd dropped off to sleep, he'd had a vague plan of getting up, cooking her breakfast and then having a long talk.

Cranking himself out of bed, protest of muscles or not, he somehow made it to his feet and headed into the other room. He was afraid that if he stopped to get dressed, she'd be gone before he could stop her.

He made it through the door and came to an abrupt halt. She'd righted the bookcase and was in the process of putting the spilled contents back on it, gathering papers and giving them a tap to neaten them.

"You don't have to do that."

She whirled around. "Good morning to you too. And I wanted to. It's a good feeling to know that I can knock over a bookcase without making someone angry."

"Never. I take it we're talking about Luke."

"Yes. That last day with him was…" Her

eyes skated down his length. "It's really hard to talk to you when you're standing there naked."

He gave her a slow smile. "Okay. Give me a sec."

He went and pulled on a pair of sweat pants and then arrived back in the room. "I want to hear the rest of the story. This is the day you got away?"

"Yes. Remember I told you he opened credit cards in my name? Well, I found out and confronted him. He flew into such a rage, screaming that I knew nothing about him. I'd seen him angry before, but this was different, and I knew I had to leave. But when I went to get Daisy, he blocked my access to her. That scared me. I backed away and went into the kitchen, dialing 911 as I went.

"I barely got out my name and address when I felt him behind me. His arm wrapped around my neck and suddenly I couldn't breathe. I knew I was going to die. All I could think about was Daisy, how I should have left long ago, how I should have protected her. Then I blacked out. There must have been a police officer right around the corner, because when I came to, somehow I was alive and Luke was on the floor. There was blood everywhere. They told me he grabbed an officer's gun as he was being arrested, and they'd had no choice but to shoot."

Zeke took a step forward. "I knew it was bad. Hell, Lind, but I didn't know it was that bad. I'll be honest. I'm glad he's dead, because I'd be tempted to put him in the ground myself."

Lindy went back to picking things up, setting another stack of papers on one of the lower shelves. He went over to stop her, to make her turn around and face him, when he recognized something she had in her hand. A small pile of printer paper that was stacked together. He saw her look at it and frown, her head tilting in question.

"Who's this?"

She turned it toward him and there, facing him, was a picture of his daughter. And not just any picture, it was one of the ones he'd been avoiding looking for. They hadn't been in his desk after all, they'd been on that bookshelf.

Every ounce of pain that he'd felt after seeing that picture roll off his printer returned in full force, and he felt himself shut down, even as her question hung in the air. What the hell was wrong with him? She'd just opened up to him and told him about the worst day of her life. So why couldn't he tell her about his?

Because he couldn't.

Maybe it was some character flaw in him, maybe he was just not built like normal people, but he knew he wasn't going to talk to her about it. Wasn't going to suggest they start seeing each other. He didn't want to watch Lindy go through what he'd put Janice through. Especially not after what she'd endured with Luke. She needed someone who could be open and honest and give her that new life she deserved. That person wasn't him.

And Daisy should have someone who wouldn't constantly compare her to a ghost or wonder what his own daughter might have looked like. He'd known all along this was a bad idea, and Lindy had shown him just how bad it could get.

"It's Marina. I used an age progression program to see what she'd look like as she grew up." He took the sheaf from her and set it on top of another stack of papers. When Lindy was gone, he was going to shred them and be rid of them once and for all.

Thank God she'd found that picture before he started something he now knew he couldn't finish. So he needed to finish it in another way.

"Listen, Lindy, about last night..." He didn't want to hurt her, although he wasn't sure that what he was going to say would do more than sting. Maybe he'd been wrong, and she really didn't care about him as a person at all. Maybe she was just experimenting with something she'd never been able to experience as a married woman.

He swallowed hard. Just a few minutes ago, as he'd lain in bed, he'd actually contemplated attaching a permanence to their relationship that had been so premature it was laughable. Except no one had ever felt less like laughing than Zeke.

"What about it?" She was watching him, a wariness in her eyes that hadn't been there a minute or two ago. Then her face cleared even as all the color drained out of it. "I see."

For several seconds no one said anything. As he was formulating the words that would make the smallest burn circle possible, she beat him to it. "Were you afraid I was going to expect something out of you because of what we did here? If so, don't. You've already seen that I'm a neurotic mess. And that won't change." She pulled her hair over one shoulder. "I have no intention of getting involved with anyone ever again. I have a daughter to protect."

The use of that last word felt designed to cut and maim, which it did. Especially since part of his reason for breaking things off was Daisy herself.

What if someday he resented the fact that Daisy was alive, and she figured out why? He couldn't do that to her. Couldn't do that to Lindy. And he definitely couldn't do it to himself.

Only he didn't need to say any of it, because Lindy was telling him she had no interest in pursuing something more. Well, that was perfect. It was win-win for both of them.

"I know you do. And I was going to suggest basically the same thing. Whether it's our timing or..." He cleared his throat. "Whatever it is, it's obvious neither of us wants a steady relationship right now. This was great. I enjoyed it. But I think we were right the first time around. It's better if we keep our relationship strictly professional."

Lindy's expression had gone very still, and he wondered for a second if he'd only heard what he'd wanted to hear. No. She'd said specifically that she had no intention of getting involved with anyone. Because of Daisy.

Well, that made two of them. He couldn't get involved with her. Because of her daughter. And because of him. She thought she was a neurotic mess. Well, his neuroses beat hers hands down.

He was suddenly wishing he'd finished getting dressed. He felt naked and exposed even with the important parts covered.

"Right. Now that we've both cleared the

air and found that we're in agreement, I'm going to go. I need to pick up Daisy from Mom's house, and I have some errands to run."

Errands that didn't involve him. The sting of pain that caused made him grit his teeth for a second or two.

"I thought she was staying with your mom for the night."

"I've changed my mind."

Because of him. A wall of hurt rose up, towering over him. "I'll get dressed and take you."

"No!" She stopped and then lowered her voice. "I really don't want them to see you pull up. It'll just give Daisy an opportunity to talk to you, and I think we both know that's not a good idea. I don't want her getting attached, only to have… Only to have to tell her that she can't see you anymore."

"I understand." His heart felt as hard as a rock. She wasn't going to let him see Daisy again. Well, why would she? It was true, Daisy had launched herself at him almost every time she'd seen him. It was better this way. For both of them. "I can at least take you to the hospital to get your car."

"Thank you, but I'd actually rather take a taxi. I've called them already, in fact. They should be here any minute. So I'm going to go down to meet them."

She glanced at the paper lying on top of the stack. "Your daughter would have been very beautiful, Zeke. I'm so sorry she's no longer with you."

And with that, she went out his front door and quietly shut it behind her.

As he stood there, staring at the space she'd once occupied, he wondered if he'd somehow just made the biggest mistake of his life. And somewhere inside the answer came: yes, he had. Only he'd realized it far too late.

Lindy got through the rest of the week in a daze. Every time she looked at the board over the nurses' desk and saw her name on cases other than Zeke's, she realized he'd shut her out. Not only out of his personal life—it also looked like he'd shut her out of his surgical life. She missed working with him. Missed talking to him. Missed making love with him.

But those were no longer viable options. So she needed to do one of two things. Suck it up and make the best of things or quit a job she'd come to love and try to find another position at one of the other hospitals in the city. It wouldn't be hard. Nurses with her qualifications were in high demand, from what she'd heard. She'd had four offers before settling on Mid Savannah Medical Center. She'd chosen the best of the best.

In more ways than one.

And it looked like she wasn't going to get to keep any of them.

What about the women's crisis center?

She'd personally asked Zeke to be involved in it. Volunteering there would be torture, although she doubted he'd put in another appearance if she were in the room.

The strange thing was, Zeke had come into that living room naked, but he'd been a much softer man than the one who'd reemerged in briefs and affirmed every reason she'd given for them not being together. Neither of them had talked about love. She'd had to assume that Zeke felt nothing for her. That had stabbed her through the heart, and she'd been unable to catch her breath for several terrifying seconds. It was like being strangled all over again. Only this time it had been caused by her own stupidity.

She could have sworn, though…

When she'd told him she couldn't think with him standing there, he'd given her this smile. This sexy, *oh, really?* kind of grin that had given her a boost of confidence. That confidence had been short-lived. Because the next thing she'd known, his face had gone stony and cold, and she had no idea why.

It had been right after she'd picked up that picture of his daughter.

Was he mad that she'd touched it? No, it hadn't seemed that way. Shocked was more like it. Well, she'd been shocked too, because the face in the top picture on the stack had looked like Zeke. So why…? Then she realized it had to do with Daisy. She was about the same age as Marina when she'd died. But what if Zeke had realized the same thing. From the look on his face it had been a while since he'd seen those pictures. Maybe he'd thought he'd lost them. They'd been mixed in with all those scattered papers.

So? How did standing here agonizing over the whys change any of it? It didn't. So it was better just to make a decision and then stand by it. The way she had as she'd stood in his living room. She was not going to go back and beg him to be in a relationship with her. The old Lindy might have done exactly that. But the woman who looked back at her in the mirror every morning was no longer a pushover who would lie down and let people wipe their feet on her. She'd made it through a terrible ordeal. This was a walk in the park compared to that.

She had a feeling she was comparing apples to oranges, but it didn't matter. What was done was done and there was no going back. For either of them. The sooner she realized that the better. With that, she opened her computer and jumped from website to website, searching for the perfect position. One that was as far from Mid Savannah Medical Center as she could get.

CHAPTER ELEVEN

HE COULDN'T BELIEVE she would leave the hospital over what had happened between them. But who could blame her, honestly? He'd done nothing to convince her to stay. He hadn't even put her on his surgical schedule. If that wasn't him telling her she wasn't wanted, he didn't know what was. He hadn't meant it that way.

No, Zeke. You never do.

But where the hell was she? The thought of her going back to California made him feel physically ill.

Why? It should make everything a whole lot easier for him, but it didn't. He was more miserable than he'd ever been, actually.

He jiggled his pencil between his fingers and tried to reason through things. Tried to take them apart and examine them one piece at a time. When he came to the one in the middle he stopped. Stared at it with eyes that finally had the blinders stripped away. He loved her.

It was that simple. And that complicated.

That was why he'd taken her off his rotation. Why he instinctively knew that things could never go back to the way they used to be. It was far too late for that. It was either all or it was nothing. And for days now he'd teetered between two worlds. The present. And the past. He could only live in one or the other.

Which did he choose?

The possibility of living with a deep well of pain with a margin of happiness? Or living with a deep well of pain and no happiness?

Did he want wrinkles? Or crinkles?

Did it even matter? She was gone. He'd driven her away with his stupidity.

There was only one thing to do. He walked out of the hospital, got into his car and headed home. Once there, he took the thin batch of papers and stared at them one by one, inspecting each change with a surgeon's eyes.

They weren't his daughter. They would never be his daughter. In holding on to something that wasn't real, he'd probably destroyed the best thing that had happened to him since Marina's death. Lindy. And Daisy. He loved that little girl. He didn't know how or why, but he did. And, by God, he loved her mother too.

Marina would be horrified at how long he'd held on to those fake pictures. The ones he needed to cherish were the ones that were real and depicted her as she had been. A sweet, kind soul who hadn't deserved what had happened.

And neither had Lindy. She hadn't deserved what he'd dished out. Or what he hadn't dished out, actually. His silence about the real issue had spoken volumes. And he'd been wrong.

What could he do about it now?

For one thing, he would get rid of these images. Even as he thought it, he turned on the shredder and slowly fed the manufactured photos through it.

Then he could learn to talk. Even when he was in pain. So what if he didn't want to. It was what adults did, and if he couldn't figure out how it worked, then he'd better damn well find a therapist who could help him get there.

One thing he did know. He wanted his future to include Lindy and Daisy.

And if he gave in and begged Lindy to come back, what then? What if Daisy got sick and died? What if Lindy was hit by a car? And died?

Was the hurt of that possibility worse than the hurt of losing Lindy forever?

No. It wasn't.

So he needed to find her and quickly. Before it was too late. And he knew just where to start.

Lindy sat in the waiting room of a step-down hospital on the other side of the city from Mid Savannah. She hated it. Didn't like the people, didn't like the feeling she got when she came through those double doors. She knew it had nothing to do with the hospital, though, and everything to do with her.

Because she hadn't liked any of the other four hospitals she'd applied at either. Two of them had offered to hire her on the spot. But she'd held off. She'd know it when it was right.

Or at least that's what she'd told herself.

She wasn't as sure as she'd once been. After all, she hadn't been willing to go back and confront Zeke about what had happened in his living room a week ago. And it was too late now. She'd already resigned from her position. She doubted they would take her back, since she'd given hardly any notice. But she'd barely been scheduled for any surgeries either. She didn't want to just sit around and do nothing. That wasn't the way she operated.

Ha! So she operated by running away from her problems? Since when? Lord, she hadn't run when she should have, and now she'd run when she shouldn't have. She'd run away from a man who meant the world to her. Who had shown her life in a whole new way. He was the best thing to ever happen to her. And she'd crumpled up her broken heart and tossed any chance of getting him back out the window.

Except he didn't love her. He'd practically said it himself.

Only he hadn't. She'd ended up doing most of the talking, putting all kinds of words into his mouth, which he'd merely repeated. And she'd never said the one thing that might have made all the difference. If he didn't love her back, then she'd have to accept it.

But what if he did? What if, like her, he'd just been afraid to admit the truth?

Dammit, she should hunt the man down and tell him how she felt about him. If he didn't feel the same way, she'd be no worse off. She could just keep job hunting and hope that she would one day get over him.

But only if she got actual closure. Only if she heard the words come out of his mouth.

A woman came out and called her name. It was her turn to be interviewed. She stood and looked at the HR person and gave her a smile and a quiet apology, and then she turned and walked back the way she'd come.

For once in her life she was going to face down her fears and kick them in the butt. And then she was going to go and confront Zeke.

As she went through the exit, she was so intent on getting where she was going that she didn't see a man coming up on her right until he said her name.

The voice was familiar. Too familiar. She turned in a rush and saw Zeke standing there. How in the world…?

Maybe he was picking something up. He might not have come looking for her. But hadn't she been about to go try to find him?

Well, here he was.

She was just going to do it and to hell with the consequences. Up went her chin and when she spoke her voice didn't quaver. Instead it was solid with conviction.

"I was actually getting ready to go see you."

He smiled. "Well, that's pretty convenient, because I was coming to see you."

"What? How?"

"What do you mean, how?"

"I mean how did you know where I was?"

He reached a hand out and then seemed to think better of it. "You weren't home and weren't taking my calls, so I went to the one person who would know where I could find you."

"My mom."

"Yes, but don't blame her. She wasn't sure about telling me at first, but Daisy vouched for me."

That made her laugh. "Of course she did. She probably ran up to you and gave you a kiss, didn't she?"

"How did you know?" He shoved his hands in his pockets. "I did something bad, though, while I was there. I told Daisy a secret."

Foreboding swept over her and then came tears, her voice breaking as she forced out the words. "Don't you make her fall for you the way you made *me* fall for you. Not unless you intend to follow through."

He frowned but didn't say anything. Okay, she'd said her piece. That was that.

"What…what did you say?" His voice was soft and laced with an intensity that sent goosebumps skittering up her spine.

She didn't care. She was going to get her closure if she had to drag it out of him. "I said I fell for you."

There. Digest that!

"What if I told you that I fell for you long before you fell for me?"

"I'd say that was impossible." Her heart warred with her mind for several long seconds before one of them came out the victor.

"Why do you say that?"

"Because I fell for you while we were sitting on a blanket at the jazz festival."

His eyes closed for a second before flicking open and staring at her. "Say that again."

"I fell in love with you." She changed the tense to present. "I *am* in love with you."

"You said you had no intention of getting involved with anyone."

"You fed me that same line."

"I lied." Their voices marched across the space in unison.

This time Lindy got there first. "But why?"

"I lost my daughter. And I was afraid of getting attached to Daisy. To you. And then losing one or both of you too. Or shutting down emotionally and then losing one or both of you. In my mind, the outcome was always the same. I lost you."

"Oh, God, Zeke. When I think of what could have happened…"

"I know. And when you left the hospital, I had visions of you running back to California and realized the real danger of losing you didn't come from the outside. It came from me. I pushed you away before you could leave. And it evidently worked."

"Not quite. Because as I was sitting here, waiting for an interview, I realized that I'm done running. Done being afraid of what might happen. Things happen, they happened to both of us, but that doesn't mean they will again."

Zeke nodded, and he cupped her face with hands that shook. "I think I finally came to terms with that over the last couple of days. I love you, Lind. I want to be with you. Only you."

She pressed her forehead to his. "Yes. I want that too. All of it."

"I don't have a ring yet. There hasn't been time. But I do want you wearing my ring. If you'll say yes."

"Oh, Zeke, of course I will. And yes."

"I want to do it right this time. My ex-wife and I got married young. Probably too young. But you and I have both lived through some terrible circumstances. And I think we're mature enough—and smart enough—to know what we want out of life and to go after it. At least I am."

"Me too."

Lindy drew in a deep breath and held it for a second before allowing all the past hurts to flow out and disappear into the atmosphere. "So are you saying you actually *want* me as your wife, Dr. Bruen?"

"I definitely do, Surgical Nurse Franklin."

He kissed her and then drew her into his arms and held her tight. "I almost lost you."

"No, you didn't. Like I said, I was coming to find you. I was planning to tell you how I felt about you. Instead, you found me."

"Thank God we both came to our senses. Is it too early to tell your folks? To tell Daisy?"

"To be honest, I think my mom already knows. And if I know my daughter, Daisy probably knows you're here to stay."

"And I am. Here to stay." He wrapped an arm around her waist as they walked toward the exit. "Come back to Mid Savannah. We all want you back."

"I don't know if they'll have me back."

He smiled and drew her closer. "I'm pretty sure you'll be welcomed back with open arms. By Neil. By our team. By me. *Especially* by me."

As the automatic doors swept open, dropping them right into the heat and humidity that defined Savannah, she couldn't think of any place she'd rather be than with this man. And now that she had him, she was never letting him go again.

They deserved a fresh start and a happy ending. And it looked like this gentle southern city was going to give them exactly what they wished for.

EPILOGUE

Lindy and Zeke, along with the hospital administrator and a few other key folks, gathered around a wide red ribbon that stretched across a white-pillared porch. What had once been a genteel old house a few blocks from the hospital was about to become the Mid Savannah Women's Crisis Center. Neil, scissors in hand to cut the ribbon, awaited a signal from somewhere off to the side.

Zeke wrapped his arm around his wife's waist, uncaring that there were photographers snapping constant pictures. His hand splayed over the side of Lindy's belly, thumb tracing over the taut surface, where a new life was rapidly making its presence known. The first three months of marriage had been exciting in more ways than one. The pink "plus" symbol that had appeared on the pregnancy test had come as quite a shock, but after a few minutes of blinding panic, he'd welcomed the news wholeheartedly.

Caleb Roger Bruen would be well loved. There were no guarantees in this life—for any of them—but Zeke had decided that fear and guilt would no longer take up residence in his heart. He had been given a second chance at love…one he probably didn't deserve, but he was not going to take it for granted, or waste a single precious minute of their time together.

"Ready?" Neil's voice called him back to the present. "One, two, three." He sheared the ribbon in two as cheers from the onlookers went up all around them.

The hospital administrator had wanted to name the place after Lindy, but she'd refused, saying that that part of her life was behind her. That while she wanted to help as many women as she could, she would rather not have a constant reminder of what she'd personally gone through. She needed to move forward with her life. Plus the fact that she wanted to be able to tell their children at a place and time of her choosing and not because they'd seen her name on a sign.

Once the pictures were done, he leaned down to her ear. "Feeling okay?"

"Perfect. You?"

"More than perfect."

She turned and faced him. "I love you, Zeke."

"I love you too."

She peered to the side, where the crisp white porch gave way to huge magnolia trees that stretched down the road almost as far as the eye could see. The blooms were magnificent. "This is my favorite time of year."

"Is it?"

"Mmm…" She put her hands on her belly. "It's the perfect time to be pregnant."

She seemed to like that word right now, and he could see why. He liked it too.

"I hadn't realized there was a perfect time."

"There isn't, but I just love the way the magnolias bloom."

He dropped a kiss on her mouth. "I love the way *you* bloom. You are glowing."

"It's the heat."

No, it wasn't, but he wasn't going to argue with her. He'd asked her to hold off working at the center until she'd had the baby, but Lindy, in her calm unruffled way, had sat him down and told him that she needed this. Needed to continue what she'd started when she'd first returned to Savannah. She promised not to take any unnecessary chances and would take a break once she hit her seventh month.

Zeke would have to trust her. He *did* trust her. She wanted this baby as much as he did. And so did Daisy. She couldn't wait to meet her new brother.

"What time do we need to be at your parents' house?"

Her head tilted to look at him as the reporters moved on to their next story and people began clearing away the ribbon and the rest of the paraphernalia that went with the grand opening.

"Not until six, why?" She gave him a smile that could only be described as wicked. "Did you have something in mind?"

He hadn't. Until she'd said that. It didn't

take much to start him thinking along those lines nowadays. Then again, Lindy had been pretty amorous herself.

"Always." He glanced down at his watch. "It's three. Does that give us enough time?"

She laughed. "Are you feeling a little ambitious today?"

"I'm 'ambitious' every day, when it comes to you."

"Well, then, I'd better put all of that ambition to work." She stretched up on tiptoe and gave him a slow kiss that made something start buzzing in his skull.

He pulled away, his breathing no longer steady. "We'd better get going if we're going to reach the house. Hopefully there are no emergencies."

She slid her fingers into his hair. "The only emergency right now…is me."

So Zeke took her hands and kissed the palm of each one, before towing her behind him on their way to the parking area. He couldn't wait to get her home. Where he could show her just how much she meant to him.

And where he would renew his vow to be

the best husband he could. Because Lindy, Daisy and now Caleb deserved the best of everything. And he was going to see that they got it.

Each and every day of his life.

* * * * *

*If you enjoyed this story, check out
these other great reads from
Tina Beckett*

The Surgeon's Surprise Baby
One Night to Change Their Lives
The Billionaire's Christmas Wish
Tempted by Dr. Patera

All available now!